MW00814526

The Military File

First Edition

Published by The Nazca Plains Corporation
Las Vegas, Nevada
2007

ISBN: 978-1-934625-21-7

Published by

The Nazca Plains Corporation ®
4640 Paradise Rd, Suite 141
Las Vegas NV 89109-8000

PUBLISHER'S NOTE
The Military File is a work of fiction created wholly by *Christopher Trevor's* imagination. All characters are fictional and any resemblance to any persons living or deceased is purely by accident. No portion of this book reflects any real person or events.

Cover, Fleshblack Images and Alexander Hafemann
Art Director, Blake Stephens

DEDICATION

For Lyle and Steve, the original "Trevor"

The Military File

File

First Edition

Christopher Trevor

CONTENTS

MILKED SOLDIER BOY

My three-day weekend of leave time was over and it was time to head back to the base, Fort Kensington in Brooklyn New York to be exact. I had spent Friday evening until Sunday afternoon in Tom's River New Jersey with my beautiful girlfriend Annette at her condo. We had watched a few movies on video, fucked each other's brains out, went out to dinner and dancing, (Annette loved the way the girls in the restaurant and the dance club seemed to be drooling over her handsome soldier boy boyfriend in his uniform, and some of the guys too, hardy, har, har, laugh, laugh) and fucked each other's brains out some more. Actually, Annette and I were like two crazed rabbits in an awful Viagra induced heat. Her car had broken down on her so she was not able to give me a ride back to the base. I didn't have a car of my own at that time so I told her not to worry or to concern herself, adding that I would hitch a ride. She was totally against that and insisted that I take a bus. "Why spend money on a bus when I can get a ride for free from someone who happens by?" I asked her. "In my uniform I look real official and non-threatening. I'm sure someone would be happy to give a soldier boy a ride."

As I went on and on at the mouth about the conveniences of hitching a ride Annette finally gave up her pleas and at around five PM I left her condo with my duffel bag over my shoulder. I was neatly dressed in my olive green colored dress uniform complete with spit shined patent leather lace-up shoes. The sun had begun setting as I stood on the deserted road waiting for a car, truck, a van, or whatever to come by. A family in a small Nissan ignored me as I held out my thumb, although the teenage girl in the back seat looked at me lustfully as they drove by. Two girls in a black Cutlass actually stopped; gawked at me a little, commented on how damned cute I looked in my soldier boy uniform, made me step up to the car and then meanly sped away. As they drove off I heard them laughing, leaving me standing there in their dust.

"Bitches!!" I yelled at them as they sped off.

A half-hour or so later my feet were hurting so I laid my duffel bag down on the ground and sat on it. I thought about going back to Annette's for a bus schedule after all, but then my luck changed, or so I thought. I looked up when I heard a vehicle approaching. I stood up, held my thumb out, and watched as a big green van pulled up next to me. The driver was a big burly guy with a beard and huge-sized hands on the steering wheel. I quickly picked up my duffel bag and rested it atop one of my broad shoulders.

"Hey Soldier boy," he said through the open window. "What a sight you are. What's your name?"

"Private Luciano!" I answered heartily and with my killer smile.

"Where are you headed Private Luciano?" he asked me.

"Brooklyn, Fort Kensington, Sir," I responded. He seemed to ponder my response, scratching his chin at the same time, really taking in the sight of me standing there on the road. Then, he stepped out of the van and came over to me. The driver of the van was easily over six feet tall and towered over me. He looked like he was built like a goddamned brick shit-house.

"Hitchhiking is against the military code Soldier boy Luciano," he said, looking at my nametag.

I told him that I wasn't looking for trouble, just a ride. He scratched his chin again and then looked at me sort of hungrily. I should have bolted right then and there. Shit, if I knew what the fuck this guy planned on doing to me I would have bolted, believe me.

"Okay Soldier boy Luciano, I'll give you a ride," he said, taking me by my upper arm and walking me quickly and somewhat roughly toward the back of the big van.

My mind reeled as he asked me what time I had to be back at the base.

"By midnight tonight Sir," I replied as he held my arm tighter and tighter and walked me to the back doors of the van.

My duffel bag was weighing on my shoulder at that point. Then, he let go of my arm and opened the back doors of his van. An overhead light in the van lit up the back interior of the vehicle. I saw that on the floor of the van were two round holes. In a corner were a pile of rope and some leather gear. I gulped hard and the big driver explained.

"Your hands will fit nicely into the holes in the floor once you're on all fours," he said calmly, as if I didn't have a choice in the matter. "Your feet and thighs will be tied together and you'll be blindfolded and gagged as well. You will ride that way all the way to your base, I'll take you all the way Soldier boy Luciano. But we will be making a few stops along the way. I have some friends along here who will want to have some fun with you." As he spoke shock registered on my handsome mug of a face and I took a few steps back from him, bad mistake.

"No, no fucking way," I said. "Look, I uh, I don't need the ride after all."

If I had been standing closer to him I would have been able to prevent him from doing what he did next. He quickly reached into one of the pockets of the jeans he was wearing, brought out what looked like a large red pellet of some kind, and threw it to the ground at my feet. The fucking thing exploded loudly and I found myself coughing, gasping and with my eyes and ears burning in as a cloud of teargas surrounded me. I dropped my duffel bag on the ground and tottered around stupidly.

"AAARRHHHHHHHHHH!!!" I gasped madly; waving my muscular arms crazily at my sides, with my burning eyes squeezed shut. Suddenly, one of my arms was grabbed tightly and I was swung around blindly till my body slammed hard against the side of the van. I opened my eyes slightly and saw the big guy looming menacingly over me. He had donned a gasmask, no doubt after he had treated me to the teargas pellet. I tried to land a knee to his crotch but the fucker was too quick for me. He pushed my hat off my head and slammed my forehead against the side of the van.

"UUHHNNFFFFFF!!!" I gasped, slid down the side of the van and fell into a stupor of sorts.

Stunned and unable to defend myself I watched from the ground as he tossed my duffel bag into the back of the van. Then, he hoisted me up off the ground like a bridegroom lifting his bride and carried me to the back of the van. He tossed me in as well. I landed on my back with my legs spread. As I sat up with my head spinning he again reached into a pocket of his jeans. I held up my hand, trying to ward off what was coming. The fucker was going to teargas me again! Standing there with that damned gasmask on he looked scarier than when he had first stopped to pick me up.

Please, no man!!" I croaked, but he threw the teargas pellet at me anyway.

It exploded between my spread legs and then I was thrashing around on the floor of the van, turning this way and that, trying to shield my eyes from the burning smoke, coughing, gasping, punching the floor of the van and kicking my feet all the over the place, all at the same fucking time.

"FUCKER, you goddamned bastard!!!" I swore like a marine, even though I'm a soldier, hardy fucking HAR, HAR!

"Heh, heh, you fucking soldier boys aren't all that hard-hitting," the guy said mockingly and just to add insult to injury he tossed another teargas pellet into the van.

"OH GAWD NO!!!" I ranted crazily as I tried to make my way out of the back of the van, but the gas masked fucker simply pushed me back in.

I landed again on my back and with my eyes squeezed shut to avoid the burning I squirmed on the floor of the vehicle and ranted and raved… A few times I managed to pry my burning peepers open and I saw that he was watching intently as I thrashed madly on the floor of the van, trying desperately to stop gagging and retching, and worst of all, to stop my poor eyes from burning. I found myself on my hands and knees at one point, my eyes closed tight as I coughed, gagged and mortifyingly farted as well. When the smoke finally cleared I sat up, rubbed my eyes and looked out at the driver as he stood there with his gas mask still on and another teargas pellet in his hand. I instantly shielded my face.

"Please man, no, no more!!" I pleaded, thinking of the training I had gone through where teargas was concerned and wishing like all fucks that I had a teargas mask right now. "Just tell me what you want!"

"Take off your uniform down to your shoes and socks," he said commandingly, sounding almost military in a way.

I looked at him through my tear soaked eyes and croaked, "WH-what???"

"Look Soldier boy Luciano, I have plenty more of these things," he said, holding up the teargas pellet. "It doesn't bother me in the least to do you over and over with them…"

"O-okay, OKAY, don't!!" I gasped and got to my knees in the confines of the van. "I-I'll do as you say man!! Please, just don't teargas me again!"

With trembling hands I undid the knot in my tie and took it off followed by my uniform jacket. As I pulled off my shirt and neatly folded my clothes, placing them atop my duffel bag I wondered if I was going to be killed out here on a lonely road in Southern New Jersey of all places. I thought of Annette and how she would feel when they found her soldier boy boyfriend's body. How I wished at that moment that I was armed.

"Nice chest Soldier boy," the guy whispered, looking at and taking in the sight of my hugely muscular chest, my giant pecs and very pointy soldier sized nipples. I stood up in the back of the van, slightly bent over to avoid hitting my head but I was still slightly dizzy. I supposed that I was still suffering aftereffects of the damned teargas. Slowly and reluctantly I unbuckled my belt, unhitched my uniform trousers, pulled down the zipper and slid them off over my shoes and black calf length socks. As I folded up my uniform trousers I heard the guy say from behind his gasmask, "Now the briefs." God, he had said it so damned calmly, as if a soldier boy's briefs was something he talked about all the damned time. I looked at him in anguish as I finished folding up my uniform pants and placed them with the rest of my uniform. I realize that at that moment I was in a shit-load of trouble but I could not help being neat and folding up my uniform as I took it off, it's my training after all. Then, I pulled my olive colored briefs down and off myself and there was no hiding it, my cock was gargantuan and hard, as hard as a fucking rock. Whenever I'm scared my cock seems to betray me by laying a hard-on. My big juicy balls were hanging down low and swinging like a goddamned pendulum between my tree-trunk like thighs. I tossed my briefs onto the stack of my discarded clothes as the driver stared in awe at my steel-like erection.

"What a meat stick you have there Private Luciano!" he quipped merrily and finally took off his gasmask. "Looks to me like you've been enjoying all of this."

As he spoke he rolled the teargas pellet between his fingers...

"L-Look Mister, I just want to get to my base, please man!" I choked pleadingly, feeling totally vulnerable and overly sexy standing there naked but for my shoes and socks and with a beefy hard-on.

"Stand at attention Soldier boy Luciano!!" he suddenly roared at me and the thought that he sounded almost military again flitted through my mind.

Without thinking about it I snapped to attention and stood rigidly still in the back of the van, the top of my head brushing the ceiling of the vehicle. Standing at attention with my rock hard cock on display just seemed wrong somehow...

"You will get to your base," he said. "I promised you a ride and you're going to get it."

He stepped up into the van and stood fearlessly next to me, giving one of my very fleshy, very pointy nipples a squeeze. It didn't seem to faze him that I was a trained soldier and that under normal circumstances I could break him in half. But at the moment with me stripped practically naked and him armed with a goddamned gas pellet he had all the advantages it would seem.

"Believe me Soldier boy, you are going to get it," he said breathlessly, squeezing the fuck out of my nipple as I moaned and my cock made like a Mexican jumping bean and bobbed around between my legs.

He looked me over with that goddamned teargas pellet in his hand as I shook in my shoes and socks. Having been tear gassed had also ruined my vision for the moment, making me all the more less able to break the fucker in half, plus I was still coughing here and there. I was in no condition for hand to hand combat at that moment. GAWD, awful feeling for a soldier boy let me tell you.

"Okay Soldier boy, at ease, my name is Lenny, that's all you need to know for the moment, lets now get you into position for your ride and get on our way," he ordered and pointed to the two holes in the floor of the van.

"Hands in those," he reminded me.

I sunk to my knees and my hands did fit into the two holes, all the way up to my wrists. Lenny leaned down and gave my upturned rump a hard slap. I yelped in pain and then watched helplessly as he squatted next to me and stuffed dirty rags into the holes all around my hands and wrists, jamming them in place in the holes. The teargas pellet was now back in the pocket of his jeans, but being that he had immobilized me he no longer needed it. Now I was most definitely not a threat to him. When he was done confining my hands he ordered me to try to pull them out of the holes and he said that I was to try with all of my soldierly strength. I did as he said, I tried, I really fucking tried, but my hands would not budge.

"Got you good Soldier boy Luciano," he said, giving my buzzed head a rub.

He then moved behind me and roped my feet tightly together. When he was done doing that he playfully snapped the elastic in my black socks a few times and ran his big hands over and over my patent leather shoes. I grimaced at his touch yet my cock twitched as it now dangled between my legs. He then tied a good length of rope around my stomach area and tied the slack to a metal bar attached to the ceiling of the van. Unbelievably my cock got harder and harder as he worked at immobilizing me more and more.

"You aren't so private anymore Private Luciano," Lenny laughed as he wedged a finger into my gaping asshole.

I yelped again in pain and then he pulled my cock and balls out from between my thighs.

"Yeah, *what a meat stick,*" he said, holding my most private pulsing organ in his hand. "What a fucking piece of meat you were blessed with Soldier boy Luciano! And just look at those succulent soldier boy nuts."

"Yeah, how about that huh?" I laughed stupidly. "My girl loves them…"

He gave my rump a hard slap and then moved in front of me again. He picked up two long strips of black leather.

"Anything else you'd like to say at the moment Soldier boy Luciano?" Lenny asked me, looking adoringly into my eyes. "I'm about to gag you."

With my lips trembling and choking back tears I asked him not to hurt me and to *please* get me to my base on time. He told me he would have me there with time to spare, plus with a little fun along the way. With that he placed the strip of leather over my mouth and tied it tightly behind my neck. Using a wet cloth he cleaned my eyes for me of the teargas. It felt refreshing and I was able to see well now. The way he cleaned my eyes was almost loving and caring in a way. Lastly, he blindfolded me with the other strip of leather. He ran his hand over the top of my head and said, "I won't ever hurt you Soldier boy Luciano." I then heard him step out of the van, close the rear doors, locking them and then he got in the driver's seat. The van began moving. I trembled in terror in the bondage and fought back tears behind my blindfold. On the upside I was headed for the base, *but what a fucked up way to pay for a ride.*

Fifteen minutes or so later Lenny stopped the van and I heard him get out of the driver's seat. The rear doors of the van opened and stepped up inside with me.

"Enjoying the ride so far Soldier boy Luciano?" he asked me.

I reluctantly nodded "yes." He then knelt behind me and I was shocked to feel his tongue moving over my balls that he had been so fascinated with. I sputtered wildly behind my gag as he lapped hungrily at my big juicy balls, my cock pulsing and stiff at the same time. Then, he closed a hand around my long hard pulsing member and gently stroked it.

"What a meat stick you've got Soldier boy Luciano," he panted, repeating again what he'd said to me a few times already. "Beautiful fucking piece of cock, how the girls must adore you!"

He stroked me faster and faster, harder and harder until finally, I shot my goddamned load of spunk. I gasped angrily behind my gag as Lenny stroked me and I seemed to come and come in gushed upon gushes. My jazz splashed onto my muscular thighs and I felt it slowly dripping down the backs of my muscular legs.

"MMMMFFFFFFFF!!!!" I gasped over and over in anger and the forced ecstasy.

My head thrashed around as the ecstasy overtook me. FUCK, this guy had just gotten my goddamned nut…

"Nice gusher Soldier boy Luciano," Lenny said, not letting go of my cock.

When I was done Lenny still didn't let go of my manhood, he continued stroking me, driving me batty. I made sounds of anguish behind my gag, hoping that he would realize I was signaling for him to stop, but the fucker didn't stop, he just kept on masturbating me. He stroked my slimy cum coated cock back up to another hard-on, hurting me somewhat erotically at the same time. A wave of pain and pleasure took over me and my head spun again.

"Oh yes Soldier boy Luciano, I am going to milk and milk you real well," Lenny teased me.

And milk me he did, just like a goddamned steer, FUCK, I shot my load a second time. My creamy juices splashed down the backs of my thighs again as I shook helplessly in ecstasy and I felt my soldier boy jazz dripping down my legs. Lenny then let go of my cock and I thought it was over. To my utter shock he slurped my semi-soft almost shriveled cock into his mouth.

"MMMFFFFFF????" I asked, my gagged and blindfolded head popping up in disbelief.

The guy, the FUCKING GUY sucked my big meat like a pro, forcing me to a new third hard-on. He caressed my aching balls at the same time and goose bumps broke out all over my muscular body. Part of me wanted him to stop because my cock was aching and spent, yet another part of me was in sheer ecstasy, an ecstasy I had never known before, not even with Annette. Lenny sucked me and sucked me and sucked me till I shot my load a third frigging time. I was sweating like crazy by then as he swallowed the small spurt of my jazz that erupted from the tip of my cock. I felt his tongue teasing my piss slit as he let my cock slip out of his mouth. It flopped against the back of my thighs, exhausted, totally fucking winded and spent. I breathed in gasps and pants.

"Oh you taste real good Soldier boy Luciano," Lenny said, giving my rump a hard slap.

"RRRMMMFFF…" I whimpered as I hung my head down and Lenny ran his fingers through the cum dripping down my thighs.

"Tell me Soldier boy Luciano, are you straight?" Lenny asked me.

I nodded that I was.

"Do you have a girlfriend?" he asked.

I nodded "Yes" again.

"Ever been with a guy before now?" he asked, caressing my bound feet.

I reluctantly nodded "Yes" and I swear I could feel his smile drinking me in.

"You and those army buddies of yours get it on eh?" he teased me. "I bet all you boys make it into games of wagers and such huh?"

I smiled behind my gag, thinking of my horny buddies and me when we played our games when Sarge was not around. Lenny said that he figured as much, adding that most guys in the military are frustrated closet cases. I resented that remark. Then, he took my shoes off my feet and ran a finger over the bottoms of my bound-socked feet. A chill coursed through me as he slightly tickled me. Thoughts of my soldier buddies tickling my damned feet flitted through my mind next and my spent cock churned.

"I have to stop at a buddies' house in about a half hour so we better get moving," Lenny said. "I know that you'll probably have to piss at some point soon. Being milked the way you were just now can do that to a man. Feel free to piss Soldier boy Luciano."

FUCK! I thought for sure that when he had mentioned my having to piss that he would undo me from the bondage. No such luck though, GAWD! I heard him step out of the van, close and lock the rear doors, and we were moving again. As Lenny drove I heard him singing a mocking song that he'd made up about me. It went something like this:

"I got me a soldier boy, his body's lean and firm, gonna teach this boy some lessons, gonna make his manhood burn! I got a handsome soldier; he's all tied up in back, my rugged soldier boy, his cock I'll constantly jack. WHOOOO!!! Oh yeah, my soldier, he's handsome but not too bright, I found him on the roadside, gassed him good, ON A DARK AND LONELY NIGHT!! WHOOOOO HOOOOO!!! SOLDIER BOY!!!"

Lenny sang his song a few times more, beating his hand against the steering wheel as he drove. I pissed twice along the way. It flowed down the backs of my legs, mixed with my caked up jazz back there and all of

18

it soaked onto my calf length black socks, humiliating! The mixture of scents, my sweat soaked socks, my cum, my sweaty torso, my jazz and piss all filled the rear of the van I was tied in. After a while more Lenny stopped the van again and I heard two male voices greeting him. After Lenny and his two friends exchanged their pleasantries and hellos he said that he had a surprise for them. Needless to say I was the surprise. Lenny opened the rear doors of the van and I heard hoots of "Oh shit, holy shit, and look at that creamy ass!!"

"He's a soldier boy," Lenny said to his two friends. "That's his uniform next to him all neatly folded on his duffel bag, including his danged briefs. The handsome prince was hitching a ride, I tear gassed the kid, hated to do it but I needed to subdue him somehow, man, I got real fucking lucky tonight."

As Lenny and his buddies gawked at me I found myself stupidly wiggling my "creamy" ass.

Lenny stepped up into the van in front of me and removed my gag and blindfold. I turned to look at his two friends.

"How did you get him all tied up like this?" one of them asked Lenny. "Did he put up a fight?"

Lenny recounted as he tear-gassed me, overpowered me and then forced me into submission. As he took a small blue pill out of his shirt pocket he went on to tell his two friends that he was taking me to my base in Brooklyn, New York. Then, Lenny meanly grabbed my chin and forced my mouth open.

"GHHAAAAHHH!!!" I gagged as he slipped the blue pill into my mouth and then forced my mouth shut.

"Swallow that Soldier boy Luciano," he seethed in my face as he held me by the chin. "And may God help you if you don't…"

I looked at him thinking he'd just poisoned me and gulped hard, forcing the pill down with no water. He let go of my chin and I squeaked out, "What was that you just gave me?" He chuckled and told me to get ready for the ride of my life, adding that he'd just force-fed me a one hundred milligram dose of Viagra. I shook my head in disbelief and then watched as his two friends picked up articles of my clothing. They sniffed my briefs, the insides of my shoes, the collar and the armpits of my uniform shirt. While they were doing that Lenny rubbed the top of my head and said that the Viagra would take effect very shortly. He wasn't kidding. I could already feel my spent cock coming back to life.

"Soldier boy, these are my two good buddies, Scott and Paul," Lenny said, again cupping my chin in his hand.

He moved my head around so that I was facing him…

"Wh-what are they going to do to me?" I asked sheepishly and in fear.

"Milk you Soldier boy Luciano," Lenny replied. "They are going to milk you! That's why I just forced that Viagra down your throat. After sperming for me three times already I figured you'd need a little help-along here. WHOOOOOOO!!!"

"Oh good God," I said softly.

And then, before I could take my next breath all three of the men started working me over at the same time. Paul slurped my cock into his mouth from behind my thighs and began sucking it in earnest, really feasting on my meat. Gawd, if you've never had your cock sucked that way I truly recommend it buds. Scott straddled me by standing over my muscular back, pushed my ass cheeks apart and leaned down to begin tonguing the fuck out of my gaping asshole. GEEZ, I had never had my ass eaten before, not by any woman or guy for that matter, but I have to say the feeling was electric as Scott at my ass juice. Lenny knelt in front of me and looked into my wide open eyes as he reached under me and began teasing and twisting my man sized nipples with his thumbs and fingers. Paul sucked me up to a new hard-on. I would guess that the Viagra that Lenny had forced me to swallow played a small part in that, but for the most-part these guys were expert at what they were presently doing. As Paul sucked me it still hurt a bit as I was aching from earlier when Lenny had forced three hefty jazz shots from me. Not to mention all the sex I'd had with Annette over the past weekend, but just for the fuck of it all I'll mention it, hardy fucking HAR, HAR, laugh, laugh! I looked up at Lenny as he squeezed my nipples harder and harder, twisting those nubs of mine like they were bottle caps.

"OHHHHH GOD," I whined at him.

A few minutes went by and then I shot my load. Paul took my cock out of his mouth and held it tightly in hand as I shot my jazz down onto my socks this time.

"OH YEAH!!! FUCKING A!!!" I screamed and ranted in a mixture of a twisted pleasure and pain.

As soon as I was done Scott abandoned my grungy asshole and moved down near my softening cock. Paul ceremoniously inserted my throbber into Scott's mouth for him.

"Suck this real handsome soldier boy," Paul said to Scott in a commanding tone of voice.

Scott did as he was told and began hungrily chowing down on my meat stick.

"OH, no, no," I begged. "I'm so sexy and vulnerable feeling after I shoot a load…"

I looked beseechingly at Lenny and asked him, pleaded with him to tell them to stop; adding that my poor cock was truly aching now. He smiled at me real evilly and continued teasing and tweaking my nipples, which by now were red and swollen.

Scott sucked me like he was trying to get the gift of eternal life from my piss hole. His goddamned mouth felt like a human vacuum cleaner as his tongue moved all over my aching cock. All the while Paul was busy licking my jazz off my socks.

"GOD, *I can't stand it,*" I rattled through clenched teeth as Scott forced me toward another gusher.

The guy pushed his tongue tip into my piss slit and then pulled my cock forcefully down into his throat. And then, oh then, I felt it as I was shooting my load yet again. That Viagra really does wonders for a guy let me tell you buds.

"OHHHRRRRRR…" I moaned heavily. "I'm going to cum you guys!! OH GAWDS!"

Scott took my cock out of his mouth and held it tightly in hand, just as Paul had as I spermed and jazzed for him.

"Oh yeah, milk that soldier boy," Lenny said. "Nothing's better than making a soldier cum over and over."

The small amount of jazz squirted downward onto my goddamned socks, mixing with Paul's saliva. I gasped wildly for breath as Lenny finally let go of my nipples. As the blood flowed and rushed back through my man sized nipples the feeling in them was electric.

"Okay guys, your turns now," Lenny said.

At Lenny's word Paul and Scott took their cocks out of their jeans and began jacking each other off slowly, In between they fed me their cocks and made me suck them, then it was back to watching them jack each other off. I watched, marveling at their huge cocks. When they shot their loads they squirted their pearly juices all over my socks too. It seemed that these guys were all foot fetishists as well as milk machines.

"OH YEAH, yeah," the two men grunted and gasped in unison as they shot pent-up monster sized loads of jazz.

"What fucking loads," I exclaimed loudly, my fascination betraying me.

As the two men shot their loads and swore like marines and panted they reached down to give my very on display rump a few sexy slaps each, getting a few yelps out of yours truly here. When they were done they slipped their cocks back into their jeans and stepped down and out of the van. Lenny put the gag back over my mouth and blindfolded me again also. He stepped out of the van and I heard him saying good-bye to his two friends. The rear doors of the van closed and we were again on our way toward Fort Kensington.

What a position I was in. I wondered if any of my buddies had ever paid for a ride in the way I was paying, with my goddamned sperm of all things. My cock felt like a numb lump of skin as it dangled all soft and shriveled now, overly used, behind my thighs. My knees were sore from the position I was tied in and my nipples felt sore from the way Lenny had teased, pinched and twisted them. Miraculously my cock got hard again as I thought about these things. Was I just a glutton for sexual punishment?

Later, the van stopped again and I heard Lenny get out. I shuddered as it was obviously milking time for me again. The rear doors opened and Lenny stepped in behind me.

"Nice hard-on Soldier boy Luciano," he said, giving my rump a hard slap. "I knew you would be hard again in no time. That Viagra I gave you and milking you over and over keeps you in a state of sexual tension."

He sat down next to me and gently stroked my hard cock a few times.

"We're almost to your base now Soldier boy Luciano," Lenny said, sounding sad. "This will be the last time I milk you. Then I'll untie you and you can get back into that regal looking uniform of yours."

Milk me again?!? I could not believe it. Did I actually have enough jazz in me for the kind of abuse he was heaping on me? Well, like it or not I was about to find out. I felt some kind of lubricant being rubbed onto my cock.

"I'll lube you up good, real well," Lenny said. "Besides the Viagra it'll make it easier for you."

Then, when my hard, sore cock was totally lubricated Lenny grabbed it in hand and began stroking it, hard and fucking fast.

"*RRRRRmmmmmmmfffff!!!!*" I bawled as my head shot up in the air.

Dizziness set in and I was having trouble breathing, but Lenny was relentless as he stroked and stroked me toward yet another gusher. It felt like he was stroking everything I had in me out through my lubed up hard cock. Unbelievably I felt myself shooting my load for what seemed like the thousandth time that night. It looked like the Viagra was still working its magic on me. My jazz again landed on my socks.

"Oh yes Soldier boy Luciano," Lenny teased me as he twirled my cock. "When you get back to your base you had better change those socks. They're telling a story or two at this point."

My body writhed, my muscles flexed involuntarily and I shook like a leaf as Lenny squeezed the last remnants of cum from my cock. He then began not sucking me, but suctioning me. In moments I was drenched in sweat as he mouthed me to another raging hard-on. If I had not been gagged I would have screamed for him to stop, although I doubt that he would have. Lenny ran his hands over my thighs as he forced me to cum, *and I did.* I came again but Lenny swallowed the tiny droplet of jazz that spurted from my tingling penis. Slowly, he let my cock slip out of his mouth and without a word he stepped out of the van and closed the doors. I heard him get in the driver's seat and then the van was moving again…

At eleven fifteen PM we arrived at the front gates of Fort Kensington. I had forty five minutes to spare. The rear doors of the van opened and Lenny stepped in.

"You're home Soldier boy Luciano," Lenny said, giving my upturned rump a hard slap.

He knelt in front of me and took the blindfold and gag off me. I looked up at him and without thinking about it I puckered my lips. He cupped my chin in his hand, something he seemed to love doing, leaned down and kissed me gently on the lips over and over again. He ran his hand gently over my buzzed cut hair as he kissed me and kissed me and kissed me, caressing and squeezing the back of my big neck as well.

"Oh God, my beautiful soldier boy, what am I going to do with you now?" he asked, his lips mere inches from mine as he asked me.

"D-don't leave me Lenny," I whispered hoarsely and he kissed me again, harder this time, and more roughly.

"But I have to," he replied. "Otherwise we'll both be in a shit-load of trouble. You see, I have my base to get too also."

I looked up at him in shock as he took the rags out of the holes and I slowly pulled my sweaty hands out.

"Y-your base?" I asked him in disbelief.

"Yes Private Luciano, I'm Sergeant Leonard Cohen, United States army," Lenny said. "I-I'll try to visit you often."

In moments I was completely untied. Lenny, or should I say, Sergeant Cohen was sitting against the side of the van and I was seated between his muscular legs with my head against his shoulder. He was gently massaging my nipples as I held my hard (again) cock in my hand. He licked my earlobe and sucked it as well.

"Do it yourself this time Soldier boy Luciano," he whispered to me, giving the back of my head a kiss. "God almighty I'm so sorry I tear gassed you."

He held me tighter and kissed the back of my neck.

I began slowly and picked up the tempo as I went along, stroking my tired cock like crazy. To help me along Lenny, er- Sergeant Cohen squeezed my nipples hard, licked my earlobe, and kissed my neck. I came in a small squirt in my hand, moaning like crazy, pressing myself up against Sergeant Cohen. Then, I shifted position and took his cock into my mouth. I did not plan on milking him as he had done to me, but I wanted to show him my devotion, and yes, my love. When he shot his load I swallowed every last drop of him as he moaned and writhed in ecstasy. He gathered me into his arms and kissed my face, my ears, my neck and my eyes.

"You feeling okay?" he asked me, running his fingertips over my eyes. "That tear gas leave any ill feelings in your eyes? Can you see okay?"

I smiled at him and said that I was okay...

Finally, I collected myself, wiped as much of the cum off my black socks as possible and put my uniform back on. I stepped out of the van fully dressed and picked up my duffel bag. Sergeant Cohen stepped out of the van with me and I stood at attention before him. He straightened my tie and gently patted my face.

"I'll try to come here on weekends to see you, if possible Private Luciano," he said as I stood at soldierly attention. "Would that be okay with you?"

"Yes Sir," I said. "It would be fine with me Sir!"

With that I watched him get in his van and drive away. I stood there till I could not see the van anymore. Then, with tears in my eyes, my duffel bag in hand and a sore cock in my pants I walked slowly into Fort Kensington.

I still see Annette on my allotted leave time, but most of my free time on the base is spent in secret with Sergeant Leonard Cohen, being milked...

A Boner Book

TICKLING THE SOLDIER

Author's Note and Dedications: At this point in time I have written, had published, started to write, am working on and had so many tickle stories inspired by so many different guys (and some women as well), that I thought for this one, "Tickling The Soldier", it was high-time I dedicated a tickle story to the guys who have been there for me since all this tickling madness began. I also felt that with my combined fetishes for "Military Uniforms" and "Tickling" this would be the most superb time for a multi-dedication. So, with that in mind I hereby dedicate the story, "Tickling the Soldier" to the following and very best tickle buddies any guy could have the good fortune to know:

Rich (AKA Catinhat): much thanks for posting my work on your awesome website "MyFriendsFeet.com" and for the video "Tickling the Pitcher." Rich, I fell in love with you in the "Signs of a Struggle" video. "Oh yeah, work those feet."

Mr. Nightlinger: thank you to you as well for posting my stories on "Myfriendsfeet.com."

ETUK: The tickler of handsome Wall Street executives.

Wayne: The sheer socked tickler.

Tim Backman: Ever the tickle hero, in both worlds of fiction and non-fiction.

Tom Z: The very ticklish tickled man.

Doug Gaines: For putting us where we belong in the "Fraternity."

Wayne Courtois: A fellow tickle author. Thank you for "My Name is Rand."

Steve Sam: the ticklish executive.

Daryll: The fiendish lick tickler. Thanks for introducing me to

Neil.

Neil: The best pedicure and foot buddy a guy could know.

John: The red socked tickled guy.

Steve: Who just loves to tickle you.

Vince: For fiendish inspiration and friendship too.

Adam H: Thanks for helping to bring "Chuck's Ticklish Plight" to written life and thanks as always for your ideas and inspiration. You are a treasure my friend.

Alan: As always, my partner, for being there for me for the last 16 years. I love you.

All the guys (and girl) of "The Dinner Club": Thanks to all of you for support, thanks for believing in me and being there for me.

My name is Sommers, Ron Sommers to be exact. I'm a sergeant in the United States army and damned proud of it. I'm forty-eight years old; a career soldier I suppose you would call it. I joined up when I was nineteen. I'm married and I have two daughters. Recently I was cleaning out a closet and came across an old photo album. I dusted it off and sat down on the living room couch to look through it. In the album there were pictures of me in my uniform when I had first joined the army, twenty-nine years ago to be exact. There were pictures of me with my parents, (God, but they looked so damned proud) friends, and neighbors that I had grown up with. As I looked through the photo album I could not believe that so much time had gone by, and so quickly at that it seemed. I turned the page again and saw a caption on top of the page which read "Ron's first homecoming." It was my mother's handwriting and beneath it was a picture of me in my olive colored dress uniform, standing with my parents in front of the house we had lived in. I recalled that day vividly. I had been in the army almost a year and had been granted my first week of leave. Of course I spent it with my parent's at their house. I was their only child and they had missed me as much as I had missed them. On the next page was a picture of me with a few of the neighbors and when I turned the page again and saw the picture it felt as if my heart had stopped for a second. It was a picture of me with my four best buddies from the neighborhood. Their names were Eddie, Lester, Arnold and Ted. As I stared at the picture my heartbeat accelerated and suddenly, without any warning, my cock got hard in my pants. The next picture was of me sitting perched up on Eddie's shoulders, his big hands wrapped around my black socked ankles, and my other three buddies standing around us. I looked totally triumphant sitting on Eddie's shoulders. When my mother had seen Eddie hoist me to his shoulders she thought it would make a great picture. My cock pounded harder yet in my pants. I was remembering what my four so called buddies had done to me as a way of welcoming me home, and as a way of playing a very horrible joke on me. As I said, I had joined the army when I was nineteen. When I was granted my first leave I was twenty. I took a Greyhound bus to my hometown and my father picked me up at the bus terminal. He looked so proud when he saw me get off that bus, me clad in my olive colored dress uniform. We ran toward each other and hugged till it hurt.

"Damn, it's good to see you Ron," my father said, choking back tears.

"You too Dad, you too," I sniffled as he held me, my tears streaming out of my eyes, his hand on the back of my neck.

He drove us home and when we pulled up in front of the house I saw that my mother and a few of the neighbors were there, waiting for us. Before I could get my duffel bag out of the trunk of the car I was hugged, kissed, and hugged even more by the older women of the neighborhood. Even some of the young girls came to welcome me home. Some of them kissed me more than once, their lips really pressing hard against my face. I wondered if they were leaving lipstick smears on me. I felt like a damned war hero. My mother cried as she hugged and kissed me over and over. She was acting as if I had been gone for years or had been to war. But then, I was her little boy after all. We took a few pictures in front of the house and slowly the neighbors started dispersing.

"I didn't expect all this fanfare," I said to my parents. "I feel like I'm returning from a war or something."

"Well, when I told everyone you were coming home they were all very anxious to see you," my mother said proudly.

"Yeah, I gathered that," I said as I wiped lipstick off my face with my fingers, smiling like a kid.

"Well, let's go in and have lunch," my mother said. "I have all your favorite dishes ready for you."

"Okay, you and Dad go on in," I said. "I just have to get my duffel bag out of the trunk."

As they went in the house I opened the trunk and hauled out my big duffel bag. Suddenly, from behind I heard someone letting out a loud whooping sound of sorts. I dropped my duffel bag on the ground and quickly turned around, but not quickly enough to prevent my buddy Eddie from charging up to me, sliding under my legs, and hoisting me up off the ground and to his big shoulders.

"UHHHNNNNFFF," I gasped as my feet left the ground and I was hoisted high and quickly balanced up there.

"WHOOOOO!!!" Eddie howled happily. "Welcome home Ronnie

boy!!"

Looking down I saw that my other buddies, Lester, Arnold and Ted were there also.

"H-hey you guys," I said a little shakily, afraid that Eddie was going to drop me as he got me well positioned atop his shoulders. "G-good to see all of you."

They weren't so much my buddies as they were the neighborhood bullies. And man did they delight in bullying me every chance they could get. Mostly because I was the little guy on the block and they were all bigger than I was. Seems like that is the law of the jungle when it comes to neighborhood kids huh? But now the tables had been turned. I was a well-trained soldier and could swat them like flies if they tried to give me any trouble. I had no idea at that moment just how much trouble they planned on giving me. Eddie and Lester were both pretty big and muscular guys with dark hair and dark eyes. Arnold had blond hair and was kind of chunky and Ted was tall with light brown hair and sinister looking eyes. At the time of my first leave I had a body like iron, thanks to all the basic training I had gone through. Eddie spun around a few times while still holding me atop his huge shoulders, his hands gripping my black socked ankles firmly.

"Ed-Eddie, easy man!!" I yelled, fearful that he would let go of my ankles and send me sprawling on my back to the ground. "Be careful."

"Yeah Eddie, he's only home for a few days and we don't want to send him back to Uncle Sam all broken and ruined," Lester said mockingly.

Just then my mother came back over with her camera and asked if we all wouldn't mind posing for a picture or two with me atop Eddie's shoulders.

"Mom, please, just make it quick," I said as politely as I could to her. "I-I'm getting dizzy up here."

Lester, Arnold and Ted gathered around Eddie and we all smiled for my mother's camera. She took two pictures and then walked back to the house, thanking us as she went. Eddie finally put me down and I smoothed my uniform jacket and straightened my tie.

"So, you're looking pretty damned good Private Sommers," Eddie said, jiggling the nametag on my jacket. "The army must be treating you right."

"Yeah, they're treating me as well as can be expected," I replied. "How are things with you guys?"

"Pretty good," Arnold replied.

I could tell he was lying just by the way his voice sounded. The four of them were the laziest guys I had ever known in my life, the kind that would never amount to anything.

"We should all hang out one night before you have to leave to go back to your base," Ted suggested. "Why don't you invite us over?"

"Yeah sure," I said, not really meaning it at all. "We could bullshit over a few beers."

"Soldier boys like beer eh?" Eddie asked me and squeezed my shoulder.

"Yeah, we do," I said and picked up my duffel bag. "Listen, it was great to see all of you but I want to go inside and eat now. I'll talk to you guys soon."

As I walked toward the house I could feel their eyes on my back. Had I known what they were planning for me at that moment I would have been on the first Greyhound back to my base. No United States soldier should ever have to endure what those four bastards put me through.

Two days later my parents decided to go out to a late movie. Actually, I think it was my dad's idea because he felt that I needed some time by myself. He was right. So, at around eight-thirty PM I kissed my parents good-bye and told them to enjoy the movie. With the house all to myself I decided to chug a few beers, watch some television in my room, and then conk out for a long night's sleep. I didn't know at that moment that I would not be getting much sleep at all that night. I stripped out of my casual army khakis down to my white briefs and calf length black nylon dress socks, got a few beers from the refrigerator and walked up to my room. As I passed a full-length mirror in the hallway I stopped to look at my muscular reflection.

"Fucking sexy devil you are Ronnie boy," I said to my reflection, smiled stupidly and walked to my room.

I flicked on the television set, stretched out on my bed and opened the first beer. I took a long hearty gulp and said, "Ahhhh, good," as the cold beer slid down my throat. As I watched television and drank beer my cock bulged hard in my briefs.

"Mmmmm, wonder what the chances are of having Margie from down the block stop by for a while," I murmured as I chugged down more beer. "Fucking girl couldn't stop kissing me the other day when I got home."

Thoughts of Margie filled my head as I opened the second beer and took a long hearty gulp of it. My cock had gotten even harder in my briefs, and not just rock hard, but piss hard as well. Yeah, beer will always do that to me. I finished my second beer and as I sipped the third one I began to feel really good and woozy. I had to piss like a fucking racehorse, but I would take care of that later. I actually like waiting till the last minute to drain my vein, it feels so good as relief fills me as I piss and piss like crazy.

"Oh yeah, fuckin' hot Margie," I whispered throatily as I lay back on the bed, stretching out my muscular well-toned body.

I dropped my half-full bottle of beer on the floor and conked out, cold. What I didn't know at that moment as I lay there snoring (sounding like a goddamned buzz-saw) was that my four buddies were silently climbing up the trellis on the outside of the house, *toward my open bedroom window.* (It was a warm night so I had left the window open a crack to let the air in, bad mistake, huge mistake.) Eddie was the first one to get to my window and when he saw the empty beer bottles and me conked out cold he gave the other three guys a thumbs-up sign. They were about to give the soldier boy a welcome home celebration he would not soon forget. Silently, Eddie slowly pushed my window the rest of the way open and climbed into my bedroom, followed by Lester, Arnold, and lastly Ted, who had a backpack in his hand. Eddie pressed his index finger against his lips, indicating for all of them to be silent. They tiptoed over to my bed and stood two of them on each side of me as I lay there slumbering. In my drunken induced sleep I heard them whispering about me. I didn't react because I thought I was having some kind of sleazy dream. The two and a half beers had seemed to have taken a strong toll on me.

"Damn, Sommers looks fucking great since he joined the goddamned army, he's built like a bull," Lester whispered as he stared down at me.

"And look at the size of those nipples on him, Gawd, bigger tit tips than a woman's…"

"Forget his tits man, look at the size of that fucking bulge in his briefs," Arnold whispered breathlessly. "Fuckin' cock of his is pulsing with a life of its own."

"Both of you forget all that," Ted whispered as he knelt at one of my black socked feet and inhaled deeply. "These big feet of his look like they're size fucking eleven, and they sure as hell smell funky."

"Listen you guys," Eddie whispered, taking on an air of authority. "If we're going to get this party going we have to get Private Sommers here roped up, and tight. Ted, get some rope out of that backpack and let's get started."

I squirmed a bit in my sleep at the sound of Eddie saying they were going to rope me up. The four men all stood silently and they did not even breathe till they were sure I was totally conked out again. Watching me squirm made a couple of their cocks' stir I'm sure. When they were sure I was in dreamland again Ted smiled, opened his backpack and pulled out some rope. As they slowly, methodically and carefully twined rope around my wrists and ankles I stirred again in my drunken induced sleep.

"Mmmmmmmhhhh," I murmured as I began to slowly wake up, in full this time.

"Hurry up you guys," Eddie whispered harshly.

Quickly, they secured the ropes around my wrists and ankles and then tied the slack of them to my headboard and footboard.

"Mmmmmmmmhhhh, wh-whass goin' on?" I slurred as I woke up, slowly opening my eyes, and by then it was too late to do anything.

When I fully opened my eyes I found myself tightly tied to my bed in a sexy spread eagle position.

"WH-what the fuck???" I gasped when I tried to sit up and then saw my four so-called buddies in my room. "Eddie!! *You fuckers, you fucking guys!!!* Some things never change do they?"

I thrashed wildly on my bed, trying desperately to get untied.

"AAARRRRHHHH GAWD, *fuckers got me tied to my damned bed,"* I seethed and my cock pounded (filled to overflowing with piss and jazz) like crazy in my white cotton briefs. "What's the point of all this???"

"We just want to give you a welcome home that you'll remember for all time Ronnie boy," Eddie said, opening up one of my bottles of beer.

"Fucker, you gave me that when you hoisted me up on your mammoth-sized shoulders and nearly dropped me on the sidewalk the other day," I spat up at Eddie as he sat down on the bed next to me.

Then, he lifted my head up and put the open bottle of beer to my lips.

"Drink up Soldier boy," Eddie said commandingly.

With no choice but to do as I was told I chugged the beer down. When I looked at my bound-socked feet and saw Ted sniffing heartily at one of them I pulled my lips off the bottle. Some beer spilled onto my chest but I really didn't give a fuck at that moment. I mean, a guy was sniffing my goddamned foot after all.

"WH-what the fuck is *he* doing???" I blurted angrily and in utter disbelief. "Fucking sleazy bastard is sniffing my rancid feet!!"

"That isn't all we're going to do to your feet Soldier," Ted said fiendishly and reached into his backpack.

He took out two Q-tips, and holding them together began running the tips of them over the bottom of my foot that he was kneeling by.

"UHHHHHH!!! Ha, ha, ha, ha!!!" I gasped as I bucked wildly on the bed. "F-fucker is tickling my damned foot!! SH-shit!! HA, ha, ha, ha, ha, ha, ha, ha, ha, ha, ha, ha!!!! *Ohhhhh fuck!!!*"

Smiling eagerly Arnold knelt at my other bound foot, grabbed it at the ankle, and pressed two fingertips against the meaty bottom of it.

"OHHHHHHHRRR no, *no!!!*" I pleaded miserably. "N-not you too Arnold!!!"

Arnold pressed his fingertips against the bottom of my foot and began running and strumming them up and down, up and down, and up and down, tickling me like crazy.

"OHHHHHRRRR you crazy fuckers!! HA, ha, ha, ha, ha, ha, ha, ha, ha!!!" I laughed helplessly. "HA, ha, ha, ha, ha, ha, ha, ha, ha, ha, ha, HOOOOOOO, ha!!! PL-please stop, HAHAHAHAHAHAHAHAHAHAHAHA!!!!!"

"Tickle those tootsies of his good you guys," Eddie said as he put the bottle of beer down on my night table and pressed his fingertips into one of my hairy and sweaty armpits.

He looked down at me meanly and fiendishly.

"Soldier boy, we are going to tickle torture you till you can't take it," Eddie said, practically drooling over me. *And then we're going to tickle torture you some more just for the fucking fun of it.*

"NO, no, oh GAWD, ha, ha, ha, ha, ha, ha, ha, ha, ha, ha, ha!!!" I roared uncontrollably. "Y-you fucking shit heads!!! HAHAHAHAHAHAHAHAHAHAHA!!!"

Lester sat down on the bed near my other bushy armpit and pressed his fingertips into it. Then, he and Eddie began tickle torturing my armpits as Arnold and Ted tickled my feet.

"OOOHHHHRRRR HA, ha, ha, ha, ha, ha, ha, ha, ha, ha, ha, ha!!!" I laughed loudly. "M-my parents are d-downstairs!! Th-they'll hear." I gasped miserably.

"No they're not," Eddie said, taunting me, leering at me. "We saw them go out earlier. When we wished them a good evening they told us that they were going to a late movie and then out to a late dinner. Soldier boy, you are ours for the next few hours and then some."

Eddie went on tickling my armpit like crazy; really pressing his fingers into the sweaty crevices in there and then leaned down and kissed me on the lips. I looked up at him in total disbelief.

"Bastards!!" I yelled in between laughing. "Y-you guys went from being bullies to being faggots!!"

Within minutes I was sweating miserably as the four men tickled my feet and my armpits at the same time. My cock was throbbing long and hard, beefy in my briefs, dribbling beads and beads of piss.

"HA, ha, ha, ha, ha, ha, ha, ha, ha!!" I laughed loudly and wildly. "Faggots!!"

I watched as Ted and Arnold licked and sucked my socked feet in between tickling them. They ran their tongues all over the arches and sides of my feet and really went to town sucking the sweat out of my socked toes. Every fucking time those two perverts sucked my toes they had looks of ecstasy on their faces. When Ted tired of tickling me with the Q-tips he tossed them aside and took a feather duster out of his backpack. He stood up and ran the feather duster over my stomach and ribs as Lester and Eddie went on tickling my now sweaty and stinking armpits and Arnold continued tickling one of my feet. I bucked up and down on the bed, laughing loudly as Ted ran the feather duster over my torso. When he touched my very erect and large nipples with it I really howled and went into frenzy.

"Ha, ha, ha, ha, ha, ha, ha, ha, ha!!!" I roared as Ted noticed the effect that tickling my nipples was having on me. "OHHHRRRR SHIT!!!"

The other guys stopped tickling me (momentarily) and stood and watched as Ted slowly ran the feather duster over my nipples. My cock was throbbing wildly now. *I had to fucking piss!!!*

"G-guys plea-please, no more," I grunted as I lay there sweating and heaving, catching my breath. "I-I have to piss like you would not believe!! I drank a few beers before you pranksters captured my sexy ass like this…and that always makes me have to piss like a racehorse… so please…"

Ted stopped running the feather duster over my nipples and the four guys looked down at me, a gloating expression in all their eyes.

"Piss?" Eddie asked me with a wicked smile. "Soldier boy, we aren't untying you for a *long fucking time* so you're either going to hold that piss *or* you're just going to have to piss into those sexy briefs you've got on."

"RRRRRRRR!!! FUCKERS!!!" I roared and thrashed wildly on the bed, trying more than desperately at that point to get myself untied.

The four men laughed at my peril and Ted reached into his backpack again.

"Oh no, no," I murmured helplessly. *"What now?"*

With a wicked grin on his face Ted held up two toothbrushes.

"Gentlemen, shall we resume tickling this hot soldier boy?" Ted asked and handed Arnold one of the toothbrushes.

"Oh no, no, no," I said miserably as Ted and Arnold settled back at my feet and Eddie and Lester readied themselves at my armpits. *"Fucking bastards!"*

All at once they started tickling me again. Ted and Arnold ran the bristles of the toothbrushes up and down the bottoms of my socked feet as Eddie and Lester pressed their fingertips into my armpits, twirling them around in there, really driving me crazy.

"AAARRRGGHHH HA, ha, ha, ha, ha, ha, ha, ha, ha, ha, ha, ha, ha, ha!!!!" I laughed and howled uncontrollably. "HA, HA, HA, HA, HA, HA, HA, HA, HA, HAR, HAR, HAR, HAR, OHHHRRRR you bastards!"

My muscular body bucked up and down as they tickled me relentlessly more and more, driving me absolutely batty. Eddie reached down and squeezed one of my nipples hard as they went on and on tickling me.

"Ohhhhhh, fucking squeezing my damn tits too huh?" I asked angrily. "Ha, ha, ha, ha, ha, ha, ha, ha, ha, ha, ha, ha, ha, ha, ha!!!!" As Eddie squeezed my nipple my cock grew even harder. By now it was throbbing crazily, filled to the brink with piss and jazz. My balls were aching for release almost as much as I was. When Eddie stopped tickling my armpit and closed his mouth around my nipple that he had been squeezing I knew that I could not hold it back anymore.

"OHHHHH you faggot," I roared miserably. "Fucking guy, sucking my tits!!"

As Eddie worked my nipple with his lips, his tongue and his teeth and the other guys continued tickling the tar out of me I pissed, and pissed, and pissed, oh jeez man, I pissed right into my briefs. The way the guys were working me, teasing and sucking my tits, tickling me, I felt as if I had lost total control…and of my piss of all things at that. Very unbecoming for a soldier boy let me tell you. A big hot yellow stain grew in my briefs as I pissed like a goddamned racehorse. The scent wafted up into my nostrils and seemed to drive the guys on even more in tormenting me. I was mortified, totally humiliated, and hornier than I had ever been before in my life. After I finished pissing they stopped tickling me again (momentarily) to let me catch my breath and to give me a very much needed drink. Eddie lifted my head up off the bed and put the bottle of beer to my trembling lips. I gulped it down greedily. Arnold and Ted were sucking my socked toes, really eating and gulping down my foot stink through my socks, but I was too tired and too winded to complain about it at the moment. Besides, it did feel sort of good at that.

"Enjoying yourself?" Eddie asked when I stopped drinking the beer.

He put the bottle down on my night table and ran his hand over my short (buzz-cut) hair.

"Y-yeah, I'm having the fucking best time of my life!!" I replied as sarcastically as possible. "I just love being tied to my damned bed and being tickle tortured by childhood bullies!"

"Well then, in that case I suppose we should get on with it more then," Ted said and reached into another compartment of his backpack.

I watched as he took out four long stiff goose feathers. He handed one each to the guys and held onto one for himself. They all began running the tips and sides of the feathers aimlessly over my muscular body. They tickled my sides, my stomach and ribs, the insides and outsides of my thighs, my legs, and my armpits. I laughed loudly, but not as loudly as when they had been tickling the bottoms of my feet as well. It seemed that if they left my feet alone I could somehow tolerate the torture, somewhat. But then, Eddie and Lester ran the tips of their feathers over and around my nipples.

"UHHNNFFFFF," I grunted and bucked up and down on the bed again. "Ha, ha, ha, ha, ha, ha, ha, ha, ha, ha, ha, ha, ha!!!!"

"Man oh man, these tits of his seem to be the most sensitive part of his body," Eddie commented, teasing the tip of one of my nipples with his feather.

"Want to bet?" Ted asked and yanked my piss soaked briefs down in front, exposing my big, hard, thick and throbbing cock.

Droplets of pre cum were oozing out of my piss hole and my big hairy and sweaty balls were hanging low in my nut sac, sitting on the bed. All four of the men stopped tickling me and looked at my manhood in awe. I looked at it along with them, as if we were all studying my goddamned cock. It was pointing straight up, begging to release the mounds of jazz bottled up in it. Smiling, Ted ran the tip of his feather over my big balls and up and down the shaft of my cock.

"OHHHHHHHHRRR SHIT, shit, *shit!!!*" I roared, pressing the back of my head against my bed and looking up at the ceiling.

Tears flooded my eyes and streamed down my face, as Arnold joined Ted in tickling my cock and balls with the tips of the feathers. Eddie and Lester ran the tips of their feathers over my nipples again, teasing the tips of them. I was in an ecstasy and agony I had never known before. I laughed, cried and was sweating. I oozed pre cum from my cock slit like crazy. My breath came in gasps as I laughed harder and harder, thinking that for sure I would be driven totally crazy. At one point I really screamed good and fucking loud because Ted grabbed me by my balls and stuck the tip of the feather into my open gaping piss hole.

"AAYYYYRRRR!!!" I screamed as he twirled the tip of the feather around in my piss hole, sending spasms through my muscular body. *"AAAYYYYYRRRRR!!!"*

In seconds Ted had small beads of piss leaking out of my slit and dripping down the sides of my cock and into my thick bush of pubic hair.

"Man, this soldier wants to cum like you would not believe," Ted said, twirling the tip of the feather deeper into my slit. "I can feel these balls of his pounding in his sac."

Ted leaned down and ran his tongue over my balls a few times.

"OH YEAH, soldier boy balls," Eddie said and he and Lester dropped their feathers.

In moments Eddie, Lester and Ted were all sprawled at my cock and balls. They were taking turns sucking my cock, licking my balls, and sucking my big juicy balls as well. They licked and slathered up and down the sides of my cock and pressed the tips of their tongues into my gaping piss hole. Arnold was at the foot of my bed, licking one of my (by now raunchy smelling) feet. At one point Eddie and Lester smacked their lips together around the sides of my cock as Ted lapped hungrily at my balls.

"Ohhhhhrrrrr fuckers, driving me crazy," I whispered.

Then, as Eddie and Lester licked the sides of my throbbing cock and Ted sucked one of my balls I felt it, I was about to cum. *There was no holding it back.*

"Ohhhhhhhhrrrrr fuck, OH YEAH," I panted loudly and breathlessly as I shot one of the biggest loads of my life all over my stomach, chest and nipples. "AAAARRRHHH yeah, oh fucking A you bastards!!!"

They pressed their tongues hard against the sides of my cock, forcing every drop of soldier cum out of me. Ted lapped my balls hard, applying awful pressure to them with the tip of his tongue, causing me erotic pain. I grunted, swore, and thrashed on the bed as goose bumps broke out all over my body. Finally, when I was done shooting my load Eddie, Lester and Ted went to work licking my cum off my chest, slurping hard at my nipples at the same time, driving me even crazier. I looked down and saw Arnold *still* licking one of my feet. I caught my breath as they licked my cum off me. I was praying that they were done tormenting me and would untie me and leave. No such luck though. Making me shoot my load was just a short break from being tickle tortured.

"Okay guys, let's get those smelly socks off him and use the dry paintbrushes on his feet," Eddie said in a commanding tone of voice.

"Ohhhhhhh shit," I squeaked miserably.

They quickly untied my feet, pulled my black socks off me, and just as quickly retied my now bare feet to the footboard. A feeling of total despair overtook me as they retied my danged feet to the footboard.

"Say you guys, I'm going to keep these socks of his as a souvenir of all this," Ted said, putting my smelly socks into his backpack.

"You can have my damned stinking socks!!" I roared at Ted, my head lifted up off the bed. "Please, just untie me and *get the fuck out of here already!!!"*

But then, Ted took two big wall painting types of paintbrushes out of his backpack. It seemed to me that he had an endless slew of things in that backpack to tickle torture me with. He handed one of the paintbrushes to Arnold and again they both settled at my feet.

"Man, his bare feet *really fucking stink huh?"* Arnold asked Ted as he sniffed my foot that he was sitting at.

"They sure do," Ted replied. "And as punishment for the soldier boy's feet stinking so bad lets tickle them."

Ted and Arnold began running the bristles of the paintbrushes up and down the meaty bottoms of my big bare feet.

"OHHHHHHHRRRR nooooooo, *no!!!"* I exclaimed miserably and lowered my head back to the bed. "AAARRRGHHHHH, and here we fucking go again!! Ha, ha, ha, ha, ha, ha, ha, ha, ha, ha, ha, ha, ha, ha, ha, ha!!!!"

As Ted and Arnold tickle tortured the bottoms of my feet with the dry paintbrushes Eddie and Lester resumed tickling my sweat sopped armpits and they squeezed my nipples.

"AAARRRGHHHHHHH!!!! HA, ha, ha, ha, ha, ha, ha, ha, ha, ha, ha, ha, ha, ha, ha!!!" I roared as I bobbed up and down and up and down on the bed. "S-some friends all of you are!!"

"Ah, stop complaining Soldier boy, you love it," Ted said as he ran the bristles of his paintbrush up and down the bottom of one of my feet. "Just think about all you'll have to tell your buddies when you get back to your base."

"If, if you think I'm going to tell my soldier buddies about this you're more whacked than I thought," I sputtered. "HARHARHARHARHARHARHARHAR!!!!"

In between running the paintbrushes over my feet Ted and Arnold stole a few sucks on my toes as Eddie and Lester sucked my nipples. My cock was rock hard again and I had to piss, *again.* But that wouldn't happen for quite a while because my four so called buddies wanted me to shoot another load of soldier boy juice for them to feast on. They stopped tickling me and again went to work taking turns licking, lapping, and even sucking my giant soldier-sized cock.

"Goddamn it all," I roared miserably as they really drove me crazy slurping at my big cock. "You guys really are faggots. Look at you taking turns sucking my giant soldier-sized man-meat."

They squeezed the fuck out of my big balls and stroked my cock hard. When I came that second time I shot another giant load of jazz all over myself.

"Ohhhhhhh yeah, yeah!!!" I bellowed. *"Fuckers…"*

I lay there catching my breath and sweating profusely as they again licked my cum off my chest. Their tongues moving over me and sucking the cum off me sent rippling chills through me. When they were done Eddie gave me more beer to drink. By then my poor head was beyond spinning, but I chugged the beer down like crazy. I was thirsty, so fucking tired and so beat to shit from laughing my head off the way I had. I didn't think I could take anymore. To my blessed relief my four buddies untied me. I sat up, swung my legs off the bed, and ran madly to the bathroom. I stood over the toilet on my bare feet and pissed and pissed and pissed into the bowl. When I was done I walked back to the bedroom; my piss soaked briefs pulled back up in front of me.

"I hope you're not mad at us buddy," Eddie said as I sat down on my bed.

He handed me a beer and I saw that the rest of the guys were all holding a beer as well.

"I suppose I should be mad at all of you," I began. "I mean, this was a shitty ass thing to do to a United States soldier."

"C'mon Ronnie, we just wanted to welcome you home *and* have a little fun with you," Eddie said to me.

"Well, okay I guess," I said with a grin and then we all clinked our bottles together.

We all finished our beers and by then I was feeling very woozy and drunk. My four buddies finally left the same way that they had come in, through my bedroom window. For the rest of my leave time I made sure to close and lock my window before going to sleep…

I closed the photo album and sat there with a slight smile on my face, wondering what had become of the four of them. Where were they now? *And,* did Ted still have my socks after all these years??? With my cock hard in my pants I smiled fiendishly, remembering how my four buddies had given me a "welcome home" surprise that I will never forget.

A Boner Book

THE SHAVED AND MILKED MARINE

"OH FUCK, OH GAWD, what a shitty ass thing to be doin' to me, fucking shaving me down to the bare necessities," I grunted angrily and miserably as my four so called buddies did their dirty work. "Fucking lousy thing you guys, get a guy out of bed at two in the goddamned morning *for this shit!!!* Fucking untie me already you blasted mugs! Some good fucking buddies you four turned out to be!"

"If you're feeling bad now Geoff just think how awful you're going to be feeling come next week when you get back to your base in Boston," my buddy Dennis quipped.

He was holding one of my big pink fleshy nipples tightly and pulled up as he shaved away the hair around it. The way he was holding my nip so tightly between his thumb and first two fingers was sending a chilling sensation through my hugely muscular marine body. I struggled like a crazed marine to pull free of the binding ropes, but DAMN, it was no fucking use, they had tied me too fucking tight those good buddies of mine.

"Yes Sir, all shaved from head to fucking toe," Dennis said merrily. "Man, you are going to be smoother than a Ken doll."

"Damn it you guys, what's the point of all this?" I seethed, balling my tied hands into meaty sized fists.

"Just helping you to celebrate your first year as a jarhead marine Geoff," my buddy Howard said as he squatted at one of my bare feet, shaving the hair off my calf and stealing sucks at my big thick toes as he did so. Fuck, fuck, can you believe that shit? The fucking guy was

45

sucking my goddamned randy toes! As Howard sucked my big toe and as Dennis held my nip in a tighter yet squeeze there was no denying the sensations coursing through my muscular well-toned marine body. Oh fuck man; these guys were getting me in a damned lather. My horse-sized cock was *again* hard as a fucking rock and pointing straight up at the ceiling. GAWD, I had been milked like crazy already numerous times, so many times that I felt like a supply cow on a dairy farm. Seeing my new erection I didn't doubt that my buddies would be stroking me again very soon, and my poor cock was so fucking sore at that point that I can't even describe it to you. No woman I ever pounded the fucking fuck out of had ever made my cock so sore.

"Yeah, great, just fucking great, fucking guy is sucking my damned smelly toes," I grunted angrily. "Not only did the four of you turn practical jokers, but you all also turned faggot!!"

My name is Geoff, Corporal Geoff Austin to be exact. I am a United States marine and damned fucking proud of it let me tell you, hoo hah!!! I'm twenty-three years old. I have short cut cropped (high and tight style as we jarheads call it) brown hair, dark chestnut colored eyes and I stand five feet ten inches tall. My body is a United States marine corp. work of art, extremely muscular, well-toned, hard as fucking iron, all from the daily punishing regiment of exercises and physical training that we marines are put through. Actually, I'm built like a goddamned work of art brick shit house…

I had been home on a four day leave when what I am relating to you happened. It was my first year anniversary as a hard-core no nonsense, no fucked up marine and my commanding officer had given me a four day pass off the base to celebrate. Rather than spend my four days in the arms and cunts of whores and risk all sorts of strange diseases I decided to visit my mother and stepfather. Aren't I such a good fucking boy? HOO HAH!! My father died of liver disease when I was a teenager. After those buddies of mine managed to get the snag on me I thought how I should have spent my four days of leave in the arms and cunts of whores. At least whores didn't fancy tying up a hot American marine and shaving him from head to toe. However, either way I would have gotten my damned rocks off. With my four buddies I got more than my share of getting my rocks off. My mom and step-dad were so damned proud of me that was for sure. Even though he is my stepfather I still think of him as my dad, he's always been that good to my mom and I. Well, I took a Greyhound bus to the terminal of the town in New Jersey where my parents still lived after all these years. They were so glad to see me and so were all the folks in the neighborhood. It must have been one of the neighbors who told Dennis and my other buddies that I was in town for a visit. It was on my second night at home that what I am relating to you herein happened. It was two o'clock in the goddamned morning when the phone rang, instantly jarring me from sleep. My stepfather must have answered it on the second ring because it only rang twice. As I lay there in the darkness of my room I simply figured it had been a wrong number and rolled over to go back to sleep. I mean, who would call at two in the morning after all? A few moments later I heard light tapping on my door. I sat up under the covers, turned on the lamp on my night table and let my eyes adjust to the light.

"Yeah?" I called out.

My stepfather poked his head in the door and saw me sitting up.

"Geoff?" he said softly. "Believe it or not, there's a phone call for you."

"Who the hell is calling at two in the goddamned morning?" I asked him after glancing at the digital clock on my night table.

"It's your friend Dennis," my stepfather replied, holding out the cordless phone to me. "And he says that it's very important he speak to you."

"Shit," I rasped, threw the covers off myself and got out of bed.

Dressed in just my white briefs and olive colored calf length marine issued cotton socks I took the phone from my step dad. My cock was semi hard in my briefs, making a nice little tent in the thin cotton material.

"Dennis?" I asked hesitantly into the phone.

"Yeah man, it's me," Dennis said, sounding sort of urgent and desperate at the same time. "Sorry to wake you up at this ungodly hour man, but I sure as all fuck need you here now."

"Dennis, is something wrong?" I asked him, suddenly feeling very nervous.

"I'll show you when you get here man, please, just come, just come

Geoff," he said, sounding more than desperate at that point.

He hung up and I was left listening to the buzz of the dial tone.

"Something the matter son?" my stepfather asked me as I handed the phone back to him.

"I don't know," I said, sounding confused. "Dennis needs me to get over to his apartment, and from the sound of things he needs me there on the double."

"Did he say why?" my stepfather asked sounding unsure of what I was about to do.

"No," I replied. "But I think I had better get over there and see what kind of mess Dennis has gotten himself into this time."

With my stepfather standing there watching me I pulled my socks up, put on a pair of fatigue style pants and sat down to lace up my ankle high spit shined boots after slipping my big feet into them. When I was done lacing up my boots I stood up and took an olive colored tee shirt from my duffel bag. Before I put it on I noticed my stepfather looking at me, really drinking in the sight of me.

"Something the matter?" I asked him, standing there with my tee shirt in hand, my hairy massively muscular chest on total display.

"No, I just can't fucking believe it, my son, a goddamned marine," my stepfather said with the utmost pride and respect. "And just look at the job they did on that skinny body of yours. Shit, you are built like a brick shit house.

It gave me a good feeling when he called me son and I was glad I had done him proud. With a grin my stepfather gave one of my big pecs a hard manly slap.

"Built like a brick shit house and hairy as a goddamned ape," he said and slapped my pec again, giving it a hard and mean squeeze this time.

"Yeah, that I am," I said in agreement.

"Fuck, I bet you could take three guys with one hand tied behind your back," he said with pride and gave my other pec a hard slap and a squeeze.

"That I could Dad," I said with a grin.

"Be careful over there at Dennis' place," he said to me as I pulled on my tee shirt. "I know he's your friend and all but I also recall a time when he used to bully you."

"Dad, we were kids then, and besides, I can handle the bastard now if I have too," I replied and flexed my huge bowling-ball sized biceps.

We both laughed.

"All the same, just be careful," my stepfather said, patted me on the back and left my room.

I quickly brushed my teeth and threw some cold water on my face to wake me up a little more before leaving the house. Holding my semi hard cock in my fingers I pissed that long middle of the night stream into the toilet. Now I was ready to leave the house. It was a warm September night so I didn't bother with a jacket. I left my parent's house and trotted slowly down the few blocks to Dennis's apartment. As I was headed there I remembered what my stepfather had said about Dennis bullying me when we were kids. He and his buddies used to have a grand old time playing mean jokes on me and just making my life miserable. I suppose that because I was the youngest kid on the block made me the butt of all those mean jokes and pranks. But, as I said to my step dad, we were kids then. *Right...* The biggest mistake I made that night was leaving the house and going over to Dennis' apartment. I mean, I had been in my bed, sound asleep and then I wind up being shaved and fucking milked till I can't fucking stand it. As I said my cock was semi hard. I hadn't gotten laid in quite some time so I suppose it's safe to say that I was primed and fucking ready for a good long milking session. My big hairy nuts were at the breaking point that night, filled to capacity with young hot marine jazz. And fuck, Dennis and his buddies drained my gonads real fucking good, let me tell you. If I thought my nuts were aching and feeling blue balled before those four guys snagged and milked me, well, you can imagine how they were feeling afterwards. By the time they got done with me my poor nuts we no longer hairy either. Fuckers shaved them down too. Within five to eight minutes I was at Dennis' apartment building. I rang his doorbell and he buzzed me in. Dennis lives on the ground floor. I sprinted through the lobby and to his door where he was waiting. Dennis is about my height with blond wavy hair and blue eyes. He was wearing a pair of blue jeans, a white tee shirt and sneakers when he greeted me at the door.

"Glad you could get here so quickly man," Dennis said gratefully but softly.

"What the fuck is going on man?" I asked him just as softly as he ushered me into the apartment, closing and locking the door behind us.

I was slightly sweaty from the quick dash I had done from my parent's house to Dennis' apartment. The front of my tee shirt was wet with it as I entered further into Dennis' apartment.

"I have something here that I want to show you bud," Dennis said, taking me by my upper arm and walking me through the apartment toward his spare bedroom.

"You mean nothing is wrong?" I asked him, starting to sound angry. "You called me here to *show me something?*"

"Sure thing man, but it's important," Dennis said. "Believe me; you're going to love it."

"Dennis, the only thing I would love at this time of day is to be back in my bed," I said to him.

We got to the spare bedroom and Dennis flicked on the light. In the center of the room I saw what looked like a combination long stretch dentist's chair and barber's chair.

"What the hell is this all about Dennis?" I asked him sternly. "It's fucking two twenty AM and I am dog tired man."

"I just got this chair at one of those odd places that opened at the warehouse area near the parkway," Dennis said, stepping next to his prized possession and running his hand lovingly over the headrest at the top of it. "Whoever designed this thing must be a fucking genius. What do you think Geoff?"

"For this you had to wake me up at two AM?" I asked him angrily, taking a few steps closer to the chair. "To show me a goddamned chair?"

"Hey bud, don't get your shorts in a bunch," Dennis said snidely. "This thing is work of art and the possibilities are endless. I mean, just look at this. The arms of the thing are mobile, they move outwards to the sides."

Dennis demonstrated how the arms of the chair moved by turning a wheel on the side of the chair and suddenly a feeling of foreboding came over me. My military instincts had kicked in and suddenly I felt an intense need to be the fuck out of there.

"See that?" Dennis asked me. "You can really stretch your arms out on this thing."

The feeling of foreboding grew stronger and I was sweating even more now.

"And look at the leg-rests man," Dennis said anxiously, dashing over to the front of the chair. "Two, count them two separate leg-rests, not just a long single one like other dentist's chairs. With your legs in these babies you can really be stretched open nice and wide. Like I said bud, the possibilities are fucking endless.

At this point my heart was pounding like crazy and *I knew* that I had to get out of there.

"Very nice Dennis," I said, sounding very irritated now. "But if you don't mind I'm going to head back to my parent's house now and go back to sleep."

I turned to walk out of Dennis' spare bedroom, but when I turned I saw his three cronies there, Howard, Alex and Ronald. In a flash I recalled how *they* had also made my life a living hell when we were kids. I realized too late how things don't change all that much in life. They were on me in a microsecond. Being that I was still tired and feeling pretty sluggish there wasn't much I could do to stop them as they grabbed me by my upper and lower arms. Alex is a wiry guy with dark brown hair, cut short. His dark brown eyes are small and beady, perfect eyes for a practical joker. Ronald, Alex's best friend is a well-toned muscled guy. He spends hours in the gym everyday. He has curly black hair and deep dark eyes. Howard is lanky and tall with light brown hair and a thin mustache.

"H-HEY, wh-what the fucking fucks is going on here you guys?" I blurted angrily as they meanly yanked my hugely muscular arms behind me, twisting them up behind my back. "FUCKING let go of me you blasted mugs!!"

They hauled me back into the room and over to the chair that Dennis had called me there to see. My step-dad had been right when he said I could take three guys with one hand tied behind my back. But what he didn't count on was the fact that I needed to be fully awake and alert for it. Fuck, these three had the jump on me that was for fucking sure. Marine or not I had been had…

"Now, as I said Geoff, the possibilities of this chair are endless," Dennis went on explaining as if I wasn't a captured marine at that moment. "And as a gift to you from all of us to celebrate your first year as a marine we thought you should be the first to try it out."

"Yeah, I'm a fucking marine all right Dennis," I ranted madly, looking at the chair in fear now. "But I don't need a goddamned haircut. As you can see the barber on my base keeps me cut nice and high and tight."

"Ha, we're going to give you a lot more than a haircut buddy boy," Dennis said snidely.

"Fucking bastards," I said angrily, wondering what the hell they had in mind for me here.

All four of the guys laughed mockingly and meanly, tightening their grips on me as I struggled to no avail.

"Fuck man, those guys in the marines did a hell of a fucking job muscling you up Geoff boy," Dennis said, giving one of my pecs a squeeze through my sweaty tee shirt. "And in just one year too. Hold him tight guys; this fucking steer looks like he's stronger than a bull."

Dennis gave my upper arm a hard fucking punch and the three guys tightened their grips on me. I yelped in pain and clenched my pearly white teeth. I railed angrily and in fury in Dennis' mockingly smiling face, asking him just what the fuck he planned on doing with me. Then, the fucking guy squatted in front of me and began unlacing my ankle high boots.

"Oh fuck man, what are you mugs planning on doing with me???" I asked desperately as my boots were slid off my feet.

I watched helplessly as Dennis sniffed the insides of each of my damned boots.

"Oh fuck, damned sleazy bastard is sniffing my damned boots!!" I ranted and tried again to pull out of the other guy's grasps.

It was no use though. They had me good that was for sure. They held me super tight, holding my muscular arms twisted painfully up behind me. I grunted fiercely as Dennis set my boots down on the floor. He then proceeded to slide my fatigue pants down and off me. When he saw the hard-on I was sporting in my briefs his eyes opened gleefully.

"Fuck man, looks like we got ourselves a horny goddamned jarhead here," Dennis quipped and rubbed an open palm over my bulging crotch. "Oh man, fucking hard as a rock and throbbing like crazy in there."

"FUCKER, pervert," I seethed. "Get your goddamned hands off me Dennis! I'm not a faggot!!"

"Milk him Dennis," Alex, ever the practical joker said. "Lets get this party going."

That said, the three guys holding me hoisted me a few inches off the floor as Dennis began rubbing his palm heavily over the hard bulge in my soft cotton briefs.

"OHHHHHHH fuck, oh GAWD, you fucking bastards," I grunted throatily. "Now this is carryin' things *and me* too fucking far!!"

I dangled there with my socked toes just inches from the floor as chills coursed through my muscular body and Dennis' hand worked its damned magic.

"Goddamn it you guys," I seethed. "I-I'm gonna fucking cream like a son of a bitch into my damned under shorts! C-can't believe this shit, y-you faggots are going to make me shoot my load!!"

Dennis wrapped his hand tightly around the now pulsing hard hump in my briefs and stroked it a few times. The combination of his hand gripping my hard manhood and my cock being rubbed against my soft cotton underpants sent me into a heated frenzy.

"OHHHHHHHH SHIT, OH FUCKING A you blasted mugs!" I panted loudly as I shot a load big enough to choke a horse. "OHHHHHHH yeah, FUCKING FAGGOTS!!"

I arched my muscular back as the three guys still held me tightly by the arms. My hot creamy lathered juices filled and seeped heavily through my briefs as Dennis went on and on stroking the bejesus out of me, him forcing every possible drop of it from me.

"OHHHHHHH, FUCKING guys, got me cumming and humming like goddamned gangbusters," I garbled crazily.

When I was done Dennis slowly took his hand away from my now cum soaked and slopped underpants.

"Bastards," I whispered, looking down at Dennis as he slowly slid my cum drenched briefs off me.

My slimy cock hung there semi erect and Dennis gave my hairy, sweaty and stinking balls a slathering lick.

"AAAYYYRRR GAWD!" I heaved and my other three buddies hoisted me higher off the floor. "Strong fuckers you guys are eh? I guess you mugs have been spending some time at the gym huh?"

Dennis sniffed my cum soaked underpants and then tossed them aside with my pants. He quickly pulled my socks off my feet and then stood up.

"Man, are you in for a time here buddy boy," Dennis said to me, sounding fiendish, tossing my socks into the small pile of my clothes.

"Yeah, knowing you four I can just imagine what the fuck I'm in for," I spat at him.

With that Dennis grabbed my semi erect crank and gave it a few mean pulls.

"OHHHHHHH FUCK, easy with my cock you bastard!!" I grunted angrily.

Dennis stroked me hard and needless to say, being that I had enough spunk in me to fill a jar I shot a hefty load of marine juice mayonnaise. The way the other three guys were holding me and the way Dennis was again stroking the fuck out of my manhood made me do a stupid sexy dance for them as I neared shooting a second load…a second robust ad hearty load of marine spunk, that was for sure bud.

"OHHHHHHHHHH SHIT, fucking bastard, milking the fuck outa me here huh?" I seethed as I dangled there in the other guy's grasps. "FUCKER DENNIS, let go of my cock man, I'm all sensitive and sexy after shooting my damned load, and now, AAARRHHHHH yeah, fucking degenerates got me cumming again…of all things!!"

My cum shot all over my sweat stained tee shirt as Dennis held my cock pointed straight up. I felt my juices splashing onto my shirt and I could even feel the warmth of it against my chest under my tee shirt. As I moaned and groaned from deep inside myself Dennis let go of my slimy cock and told his buddies to get me into the chair, adding that he would get the rope…

"Th-the rope???" I exclaimed, feeling totally confused now. "Just what the fuck do you mugs have in mind??"

Howard, Alex and Ronald hoisted me up into the combination dentist and barber chair, forcing my huge arms into the mobile armrests and my tree-trunk like legs into the mobile leg-rests. In what seemed like seconds Alex was there with the rope and then I was bound tightly at the wrists, the elbows and my feet to the damned chair. Fuck, but those guys really had me in a fucked up position. When Dennis had been telling me his tirade about the chair earlier I had no fucking idea that he planned on tying me to the damned thing. Dennis then instructed his three joke-playing cronies to go and fetch the rest of the stuff they would need. When they left the room Dennis produced a pair of heavy-duty scissors from a drawer and standing over me again began cutting my sweat stained and cum drenched tee shirt off me.

"You bastard Dennis," I seethed at him, wanting to spit in his face, but in the position I was in thought better of it. "What the fuck is this all about?"

"Just having a little fun with you Jarhead," Dennis said and slowly continued slicing my shirt off me.

The tip of the scissors rubbed menacingly against my chest and chills of fear sped through me.

"Ea-easy man, don't press down too hard," I said softly.

"Relax Geoff, I won't cut you," Dennis quipped gleefully. "Jeez, all those years of us teasing and tormenting the fuck out of you when we were kids and look at what the hell happens. You leave town for a while, become a fucking bad ass, muscle headed marine and what the fuck do you get for it? More of the same from your favorite buddies, that's what you get for it Jarhead."

"Yeah, and what I get for it is milked and bound up," I seethed, struggling to get untied.

When my tee shirt was cut Dennis ripped it the rest of the way off me. So there I was, naked as the day I was born, stretched out tight and all roped up, looking real sexy somehow if I do say so myself buds. Every part of my muscular and well-toned body was available for their perverted pleasures…

Dennis turned a wheel on the side of the chair and the leg-rests were slowly pulled further apart, stretching my legs to the sides and sadly, I might add, exposing my marine bunghole.

"AAARRRHHH GAWD, easy man, I ain't no rag-doll you know," I complained.

Leering lecherously at me Dennis picked up the scissors again and grabbed one of my big fleshy nipples. The way he held my nipple so tight combined with the fact that he'd jacked me off twice sent real chills through my muscular being. Dennis moved the scissors toward my nub.

"Damn it Dennis, *d-don't!!*" I pleaded desperately.

I watched in total fear as Dennis slowly moved the scissors toward my nipple. He held the hard nub in his fingers, squeezing it tight. But instead of cutting my nipple off my chest, which is what I was sure he was about to do, he simply snipped a few hairs off my chest around my nipple. Smiling meanly Dennis leaned down, let go of my nipple and gave it a hearty slurp.

"AAAAARRRHH GAWD, you faggot," I rasped angrily, wiggling my toes and balling my fingers into huge fists.

When Howard, Alex and Ronald came back into the room carrying a large basin of steaming hot water each I shuddered to think about those perverted pleasures of theirs that I just mentioned. From a cabinet in the room Dennis produced cans of shaving cream, long mean looking sharp straight razors and classic barber's electric clipper style razors.

"Oh fuck, oh you fucking bastards, not what I'm thinking you're planning on doing to me here," I said, desperately trying to pull free of the binding ropes, my cock wagging back and forth with my efforts.

As I struggled to no avail my cock (unbelievably) grew erect again and pointed straight up at the ceiling, betraying me.

"Looks like this jarhead is hornier than we thought," Dennis quipped, grabbing a handful of my big meat stick and starting to stroke it.

"OHHHHHHH, oh please man, not again so fucking soon," I gasped.

As Dennis stroked my erection my balls bounced and flopped in the air between my legs because they had nothing to rest on the other guys set their basins of HOT water down around the chair I was trapped in. I saw Howard look hungrily at one of my big feet as he set his basin down at the end of the chair. Dennis stroked my manhood a little faster and I was breathless as Howard slathered the front of his very wet and mangy tongue over the side of one of my big ol' feet.

"FUCKERS," I seethed. "Faggots, this is just too much now!!"

"Two of you suck his tits," Dennis instructed. "I have no doubt that'll make him cum like crazy. Besides, I want to get started shaving him down. Judging from how hairy this jarhead is we have a big job ahead of us." Alex and Ronald eagerly stepped to my sides, leaned down and greedily slurped my big nipples into their mouths. They instantly began sucking the fuck out of them.

"OHHHHHRRR fuck, oh man, of all the blasted things to do to a marine," I seethed through my pearly whites.

I watched transfixed as the two fucking guys really sucked and slurped the tar out of my big nipples. GAWD, it did feel good at that I had to admit. I leaned my head forward and breathed deeply. Dennis had been right however. Having my big tits sucked drove me incredibly wild. I shot a third load like gangbusters, shooting it all over my hairy well-defined muscular chest.

"AAAARRRHHH GAWD, oh shit, SHIT, got me creaming all over again you mugs!!" I ranted.

Dennis let go of my cock, Alex and Ronald stopped suckling my nipples and all four guys watched as my big cock twitched crazily between my spread out tree-trunk like legs, shooting rope after rope of creamy marine sperm.

"OHHHHHHHH!!!" I grunted madly as I shot my load uncontrollably.

"Jeez, look at that, fucking guy is a twenty-four hour beat-off machine," Ronald laughed.

Fuck, what a sight I was all right, all stretched out naked and tied, shooting my damned load to the glee of four perverts. My step-dad had been right after all. I should never have trusted Dennis. And fuck, was I paying for it now! When I was done creaming Dennis opened another cabinet and brought out a small stack of face towels.

"Okay you guys, lets get this hunky marine shaved down real nice," Dennis said as he handed a towel each to his buddies. "We'll use these when its time to soak him down."

"You fuckers, I'll kill you mugs for this!!" I ranted, still struggling to get myself untied.

"I get the prized area guys, remember we discussed that," Dennis said to his friends and gave the chair I was roped to a hard spin.

The chair spun around a few times, getting me sort of dizzy.

"Blasted mugs!!" I ranted meanly as I spun and spun in the chair.

When it stopped and I got my bearings I saw that all four of the guys were holding the battery powered electric clipper razors I had mentioned earlier.

"Okay you guys, let's get this party started," Dennis said. "As I said, *the prized area is mine!!*"

"Sure thing Dennis, you are in charge," Howard said, settling down next to one of my outstretched legs. "But these big feet of his are the prized area for me."

Dennis squatted between my legs and Alex and Ronald took position at my outstretched arms. The sound of whirring filled the room as all four of the electric clipper razors were clicked on.

"Oh jeez you guys," I squeaked angrily.

Then, Howard got busy shaving my leg first. Alex and Ronald had a grand old time shaving the hair out of one of my bushy armpits each. And Dennis, squatting at what he had called the prize area moved the electric clipper razor slowly over my pubic bush, shaving it away as he held my semi hard cock up and out of the way by the tip. The way he held my cock sent chills through my muscular being.

"Oh fucking FUCK you guys, FUCKING TOTALLY FUCKS," I rasped loudly as tufts of my body hair landed on the floor around the chair. "I will kill all of you for this shit!!"

"Quit complaining Jarhead," Alex said, stepping behind me and running the razor through the short-cropped high and tight hair on my head. "By the time we get through with you you're going to look so hot and smooth that you'll wish we were at your base to shave you down twice a week."

Fucking bastard, by the time Alex was done shaving my hair I was no longer a high and tight hair style marine, I was a FUCKING bald marine. He teasingly patted me on the head, squeezed the top of it and even gave it a wet sloppy kiss. When he slathered his tongue across the top of my baldy dome I most definitely could have killed him. He quickly got back to shaving my armpit that he had momentarily abandoned in favor of shaving my pate. Howard was still busy shaving my left leg, working his way up from the bottom toward my muscular hairy thigh. Dennis, suffice to say was driving me batty as he held my now rock hard marine-sized cock in his hand and shaved away what he could of my pubic nest. My hairy balls hung down real low. I glanced down at the basins of steaming hot water. No doubt in mind what they were for. As soon as the guys were done shaving what they could with the electric clipper razors they would soak me down with hot water and finish the job with steam, shaving cream and straight razors. Dennis shaved the area above my crotch slowly, the feeling of the electric razor sliding over me there driving me wild.

"OHHHHHHH GAWD, you blasted bastards," I groaned, watching as mounds of my body hair littered the floor.

When Alex and Ronald had shaved all that was possible from my armpits they stepped behind me and ran their razors slowly over my outer arms, shaving away the thick dark hair there. Chills again sped through me as Dennis, (fucking guy loved my cock that was for sure) again began stroking me, while still shaving away the hair above my crotch.

"OHHHHHHHH fuck, c-c'mon Dennis," I seethed. "L-leave my damned meat stick alone already. FUCK man, y-you're goin' to make me shoot another marine-sized load."

Ignoring me, Dennis stroked me and stroked me till I shot yet another load of hot young marine spunk. I was tingling madly from head to toe at that point, every part of me feeling sensitized, my poor cock most of all.

"OHHHHHH shhhhhiiiitttt," I squealed as my slop landed on the floor between my legs, Dennis holding my throbbing pound of beef tight in his fist.

A short while later my legs, arms and crotch areas were all just about hairless. I sat there feeling totally humiliated, totally helpless and completely violated. I watched miserably as all four of the guys slowly shaved my hairy chest. My chest was a massive mess of muscles, rock fucking hard with bouncing pecs and awesome male cleavage. My four faggot captors seemed to be reveling in slowly shaving the hair off it let me tell you.

"Man, this fucking marine is hairier than a damned gorilla," Ronald commented, moving his electric clipper razor slowly around one of my huge fleshy nipples, shaving the hair methodically away from it.

"Yeah, but he won't be when we get done with him, that is for sure," Dennis said, shaving the hair away from around my belly button.

With my head leaned down I watched as my sexy chest hair slowly disappeared. GAWD ALMIGHTYS!! When the electric clipper razors were clicked off I looked down at myself and saw that all that was left of my body hair was just a thin layer.

"*Fucking bastards,*" I whispered as all four of them picked up face towels.

In unison they submerged the face towels in the basins of hot steaming water and began applying them all over my trussed up muscular body, not so much washing me down, but more like moistening me up and loosening up the thin layer of hair that remained on me. They ran the hot steamy towels liberally over my chest, in my armpits, over my not so hairy anymore wide as a doorway shoulders, all up and down my long tree-trunk like legs, the outer parts of my outstretched hugely muscled arms and crotch area. The feeling of those hot towels on my poor crotch was a mixture of painful yet somehow soothing at the same time. I continued to watch as Dennis lovingly squeezed his face towel over what was left of my pubic bush, soaking it up liberally. They steamed me down more and more a few times each, their hands and fingers lingering on my nipples, their fingertips teasing and tickling my armpits and stealing feels and squeezes of my big muscular arms. My muscles strained magnificently for the four perverts as they tightened the ropes around me and I struggled madly. It was fucking Dennis though, the goddamned ringleader who was really having the grandest of times though. The fucking fucked up bastard had thoroughly soaked up what was left of my pubic bush while holding tightly to my big cock. And would you believe it, I was fucking hard as a goddamned rock all over again in my most private sectors.

"Fuck guys, check this shit out, hairy ol' marine Geoff is horny *again,*" Dennis said mockingly and began running a fingertip over the underside of my rigid marine-sized cock.

"OHHHHHH GAWD MAN," I seethed as Dennis teased the fuck out of me.

Alex and Ronald leaned down and again slurped my big sexy

nipples into their mouths. Howard, the sleazy pervert that he is sucked my toes on my left foot, his tongue flicking teasingly over each one before he sucked it like crazy.

"I-I'll say it again you guys, I'll fucking kill all four of you for this, I sw-swear it I will you mugs!!" I grunted breathlessly as I was handled and sucked on.

I was gasping madly, the back of my bald head pressed hard against the headrest of my prison-chair and I watched as I was mauled, sucked and used like a cheap sex toy. I didn't shoot another load for quite a while. Dennis would stroke me for a few moments and then stop. Then he would start stroking me again and stop again, he was working me slowly this time; really making me crazy with it as his crazed buddies sucked me from all ends. If I was tingling madly earlier I was even more-so now. My rock hard muscular body was matted with sheens of sweat and the steaming hot water they had doused me with. Small clouds of steam rose from my well-trussed body.

"OHHHHHHH GAWD," I grunted about fifteen minutes later when I felt myself starting to get real fucking close. "G-goin' to shoot my goddamned load again you perverts!! OHHHHHH SHHHIIIITTT, yeah, fucking A, fucking faggots, goddamned fucking bastards!!"

I had lost count of how many fucking times I had shot my load at that point. I was starting to feel pretty drained and sore yet squirt after fucking squirt of jarhead scum erupted from my wide sexy slit.

"F-fucker just loves my damned joystick!!" I seethed, looking down at Dennis as he stroked me and stroked me, milking jettisons of my good stuff from me.

When I was done spewing the four guys ran their mangy hands all over me, my body now glistening even more with sweat and the steamy water I had been baptized in. The thin layer that was left of my bodily hair was thoroughly soaked and warm, primed and ready to be shaved away.

"Okay you guys, enough feeling him up, *for now,*" Dennis said snidely. "Lets start performing surgery."

"Hell of a way to refer to shaving me," I whimpered angrily.

All four of them grabbed a can of shaving cream each. I clenched my teeth and spittle flew from between them.

"You fucking perverts!" I reeled. "This is your last fucking chance, untie me now and I'll try to forget all about this!"

But in response the four guys filled their hands with shaving cream, the sound of the cream being sprayed from the cans agonizing to my ears.

"OHHHH fuck," I squeaked miserably and slammed my head against the chair's headrest. *"Please you guys..."*

Howard began, of course, at my danged feet, rubbing shaving cream over my iron-like calves, working his way slowly up my sexy legs, really having a grand time feeling me up as he went. Alex applied the cream to my outer arms and shoulders as Ronald delighted in applying the lather to my big rock-hard chest, his hands and fingers lingering teasingly on my damned nipples, outlining them so that they were left visible. Every other part of my big muscular chest was covered in frothy lather. Alex and Ronald slathered globs and globs of shaving cream into my deep stinking armpits, slightly tickling me with the tips of their fingers. Dennis was again at the prized area, rubbing shaving cream liberally over my pubic bush. When he applied it to my low hanging nut sac he wasn't exactly gentle about it. He squeezed my marine sized testicles good and hard as he applied a handful of cream to them, tugging down on them at the same fucking time.

"AARRRHHH jeez, no man, y-you're not going to shave my damned sac too are you?" I garbled in terror.

"Relax Jarhead, I promise I won't slice off too much of your manhood," Dennis laughed and then to my total disbelief he inserted two cream slicked fingers into my very visible hole.

'AAAYYYYY SSSHIIITTT, you fucking faggot!!" I squealed. "G-get your damned fingers out of my hole man!!"

But instead, Dennis slid his damned fingers just about out and then quickly back into my hole, twirling them around in there as he went.

"OHHHHH fuck, sleazy bastard, pervert," I ranted.

"Just checking to make sure you got no hair hidden up in this crevice Jarhead," Dennis teased me and finger fucked me deeper with each damned thrust.

Needless to say my marine cock rose to the occasion, good and hard and pointed straight up at the ceiling, betraying the fuck out of me. All four of the guys laughed meanly as Dennis drove me mad, finger fucking me like crazy. Alex and Ronald squeezed and twisted my nipples as Howard sucked my toes, the few areas of my body that were not covered and slathered in shaving cream. I squirmed miserably on the chair and looked despondently at the mess of my body hair all over the floor. Soon there would be more...

"Oh man, look at that hard-on you guys," Dennis said, slowly and methodically finger fucking me, driving me insane with it at that point. "Fucking Geoff must be the horniest damned stud marine on his base. Fucking guy man, can't deny that you love all this shit after all."

"N-no way you bastard," I seethed down at him.

"Need to shoot another load of GI slime muscle boy?" Dennis asked me mockingly.

"Go ahead man, do your worst," I garbled throatily.

Smiling, Dennis wrapped a shaving cream slicked hand around my damned meat pole and began slowly stroking me. Fuck, FUCK, there was denying it. I was literally in a fucking lather at that point. Between the slimy coating of my own cum and the slick shaving cream Dennis was using as he stroked me I was a mess of goose bumps.

"Should we go for another finger Jarhead?" Dennis asked me meanly and before I could respond he inserted a third finger into my danged hole.

"AAAYYYRRRR," I grunted miserably.

The combination of Dennis finger fucking me and stroking my crank, Alex and Ronald working my nips and Howard licking one of my big feet was no doubt going to have me shooting yet another load of GI slime very soon, as Dennis had so aptly stated it.

"UHHHHHHHHH, GAWD, fucking guys," I whispered angrily and breathlessly, sweating profusely and miserably under the thick layers of shaving cream.

As the shaving cream settled in all over me the four guys had a great time playing with my cock, my nipples and my damned feet. Fuck, but Howard really loved those feet of mine. The damned guy was now slathering his tongue all over the bottom of one of them. As bad as they stunk the fucking guy loved them more and more.

"OHHHHRRRRR, OH FUCK, get-getting close you scumbags,"

I panted.

By the time it was all over and the four guys sent me home I was minus my damned socks. Fucking Howard kept them as a raunchy souvenir of all this. It actually took a little while more but eventually I did shoot another load, not as hefty as the pervious ones, but another load nonetheless.

"OHHHHHHH yeah, YEAH, fucking bastards, getting my nut juice, fucking guys making me crazy with it now," I seethed as small squirts and spurts of marine spunk erupted from my slit and landed in the shaving cream all over my chest.

Dennis kept his fingers jammed deep in my hole as I spewed what was left in my nuts onto my torso. I was squealing like a stuck pig, let me tell you bud. Finally, when I was done Dennis slowly pulled his fingers from my hole.

"Okay you guys, I think the shaving cream has had enough time to settle in," Dennis said, getting to his feet. "Let's get this shave job over-with.

Alex and Ronald let go of my nipples and Howard reluctantly stopped licking my feet. All four of them picked up a long straight razor each...

Howard began slowly shaving me at the lower legs, Alex and Ronald stood at my sides, shaving what was left of the hair out of my armpits and Dennis, GAWD, he was again at the prized area. He was holding my soft and shriveled cock (God, for the first time since being captured by them I wasn't hard) and slowly shaving away what was left of my pubic nest. The sensations of the razors sliding over me had me tingling anew and I watched, feeling totally miserable. When their razors were filled with my hair they doused them in the basins and quickly resumed shaving me. Then, Dennis yanked my cock further up and looked intently into my eyes.

"Okay Jarhead, I'm going to shave these hairy ol' nuts of yours," Dennis said, rubbing the side of the razor against my family jewels. "If I were you I would stay nice and quiet. I would not want to be startled and accidentally de-nude you."

My teeth chattered and my lips trembled in total fear as Dennis slowly shaved away the hair from my nut sac. When he was done my nuts hung down now in a pink hairless sac.

"Gawd," I whispered in somewhat relief when Dennis let go of my crank.

When they were finished shaving my legs, my arms, my shoulders and my nut sac all four of them gathered around me to shave my hulking muscular chest…

And so, that was how I came to be in the position that I was in when I began this testament. Those fucking so-called buddies of mine shaved me down to the barest necessities and Dennis, that bastard milked me more times than I can even remember. When they were done shaving all my chest hair off me I was just about completely hairless. They had shaved away all the hair on my arms and shoulders, my chest, pecs and armpits, my crotch area and my nut sac and my legs and thighs, back and front. I sat there still tied as they all rubbed handfuls of slimy Witch Hazel over my newly shaved areas. Ronald delighted in shining up my baldhead. When they squeezed the Witch Hazel onto my nipples and squeezed them hard my cock again got hard. It seemed like my damned nips were the control knobs for my cock huh? Dennis quickly squatted between my legs, grabbed my hard-on with his Witch Hazel slicked fingers, meanly jammed two fingers of his other hand deep into my hole and started stroking…GAWD!!!! After I shot a tiny spurt of a load all the guys gathered around me and looked at me maniacally.

"WH-what the fuck now you blasted mugs?" I seethed.

Howard did the honors of untying my feet as Alex and Ronald untied my wrists and elbows from the chair.

"Yeah, untie me you blasted mugs, let me the fuck out of here already," I grunted, prepared to beat the tar out of each of them.

But unfortunately for me I was too tired, too milked and just too exhausted as the four guys yanked me from the chair for all but a few seconds. They pulled me up to my feet, holding tightly to my glistening Witch Hazel, slicked muscular body. Dennis stepped behind me and ran a hand over my hairy melon shaped ass globes.

"Yep, just as I thought, a hairy assed marine," Dennis quipped and gave my butt a sharp stinging slap.

"OWWWWW, you bastard," I seethed, turning my head and looking angrily at him.

"Okay you guys, get him in the chair on his stomach and let's get this job completely done," Dennis instructed.

"OHHHHHHH no, NO, fucking bastards, leave my damned hairy ass alone!!" I reeled at them as they lifted me and my feet left the floor. "Bad enough you've done what you've done already!!"

The guys hoisted me up and slammed me back down on the chair, this time on my stomach. Witch Hazel and my marine sweat splattered when my muscular body hit the chair.

"OH no, no," I whimpered as they again stretched out my arms and legs and tied me tightly to the chair.

Fucking foot-loving Howard was already slathering his tongue over the bottom of one of my feet. Once I was securely trussed back in the chair all four of the guys gathered around my upturned butt.

"Oh man, what a hot fucking ass you have Geoff," Dennis said and gave one of my succulent looking globes a tight squeeze followed by Alex and then Ronald. "Fucking great piece of ass you were blessed with that is for sure. When we get done shaving it it'll look even better, that is for sure.

Dennis turned the wheel on the side of the chair and my spread legs were pulled still further apart, dramatically exposing my damned bunghole even more.

"Oh fuck, what a side of beef this jarhead is," Ronald said and jammed two big thick fingers into my slick hole.

"AAAAYYY, GAWD," I gasped and hefted my poor butt a few inches off the chair.

My cock slipped out from under me and hung perilously inviting-like off the edge of the chair, semi hard and dripping pre cum and beads of piss. Ronald slowly slid his fingers in and out and in and out of my hole. I was sweating like crazy by then, stinking with it like the real hard-core marine that I am. When he slid his fingers out of my hole Dennis told his buddies to pick up their electric clipper razors. With my head resting on the headrest I shuddered when I heard the electric clipper razors come to buzzing life. Chills and tingles coursed through my already sensitized body as all four of the guys took turns running their razors over my hairy ass cheeks. Just for fun and to fucking torment the shit out of me they also took turns jamming their fingers (sometimes up to three at a time) deep in my hole.

"Some hole this jarhead has eh guys?" Dennis asked while three of his fingers were lodged inside of me and jiggling, fucking jiggling around in there like I can't describe.

When they finished shaving what they could of the hair off my ass with the electric razors they clicked them off and using warm water and face towels soaked up my almost hairless butt cheeks. As those bastards worked my sexy butt cheeks with the warm water and towels my cock grew (unbelievably) hard again. It dangled there against the chair long, beefy and hard. I clenched my teeth as they applied the shaving cream to my butt cheeks and began shaving them down with the straight razors. When they were done they smoothed Witch Hazel over the final shaved area of my body, really squeezing the fuck out of my sexy tight buns, driving me crazy. Dennis, leering meanly squatted and grabbed my hard cock from behind. I grunted and groaned miserably from deep in my throat as his three buddies kneaded my butt cheeks and he stroked me and stroked me and fucking stroked me some more…as I said, many times that night, GAWD!!!

It was six AM when they finally untied me… Fuck, it had taken them less than four hours to shave me completely down and milk the fuck out of me.

My arms and legs were numb after having been stretched out for so long and my poor cock was sore to the touch. I stood there docilely, being held up by my arms and being felt up all over by my four buddies. My muscular marine body glistened with sweat and the mounds of Witch Hazel that they had slathered liberally all over me.

"Lookin' real good Jarhead," Dennis said, giving my aching nuts a quick tug. "We did a real good job shaving you, even if I so say so myself."

"TUCKER, let me get dressed and get the hell out of here, *buddy,*" I said, looking at him angrily as the other guys hands continued roaming all over me, squeezing my nipples, my pecs and my ass cheeks. "You guys are lucky I'm so fucking exhausted. Otherwise I would beat the tar out of all of you!"

"Your socks are mine now," Howard said directly into my ear, his lips grazing my lobe.

"You can have my damned socks Pervert!" I seethed in his face. "All I want is to get dressed and the fuck out of here!"

At six thirty AM I walked out of Dennis' apartment building, dressed in my fatigue pants, my tee shirt, and my boots without my socks. I walked slowly back to my parents' house, wondering just how the fuck I was going to explain my baldness. Worse, how was I going to explain my completely hairless body to my buddies at the base when I got back? Fuck, Dennis and his three cronies had really done a job on me. My cock pounded long and hard in my fatigue pants as I walked home…

The next day my parents didn't see me until the afternoon so I simply explained that I had gone to the neighborhood barber and had my hair shaved off completely. I stupidly explained that I wanted to look like a real hard-core marine when I returned to the base the next day. Looking across the table at me I could see that my step-dad didn't believe me for a second. Neither he nor my mother made mention of my hairless arms… Inwardly they knew that my four buddies had once again gotten the snag on me.

On the last day of my leave I was packed and ready to go, wearing my olive colored dress uniform for the ride back to the base. After taking a shower I was itching like crazy and used a mess of after-shave lotion all over my body to relieve it. A thin layer of my body hair had already started growing back. The way I figured it, in less than a month I would again be a hairy grunt. I had about four hours before my bus was to arrive. I was sitting in the kitchen eating a sandwich when the phone rang. My mother answered it. She listened for a few moments, told whoever that she was speaking to that she would tell him and then hung up.

"Who was that?" I asked her around a mouthful of sandwich meat.

"Your friend Dennis," she replied happily. "He said he would love to see you before you leave later."

I nearly gagged on the piece of sandwich that I was about to swallow.

"He said that he wanted to see me?" I asked in disbelief.

"Yes dear," my mother replied. "He's home by himself and said that it would be great to see you one more time before you head back to your base."

"Alone?" I asked, getting to my feet and pulling my jacket on hastily. "He said that he's home alone?"

"Well yes dear," my mother replied, sounding confused now as I dashed out the door.

I sprinted down the block toward Dennis' apartment, my spit polished patent leather lace-up shoes clacking on the pavement. I was hell bent on teaching the bastard a lesson. When I got to his apartment building I saw one of the tenants just coming out of the lobby. I quickly grabbed the door before it could close and sprinted through the lobby to Dennis' door. That way he would have no warning that I was there and would not have to buzz me in. I knocked loudly. Without asking who was there Dennis opened the door.

"Hello Dennis," I said snidely and muscled my way past him and into his apartment, slamming the door behind me.

"Hey buddy, glad you came by," Dennis said happily. "I guess your mom gave you my message."

"She sure as shit did," I said, raw and unbridled anger showing in my eyes. "But I'll tell you *buddy,* you must have been crazy to have wanted to see me one more time before I left."

As I spoke I was backing the guy up against a wall.

"Why is that man?" Dennis asked me, sounding a little confused.

"After what you and those three lackeys of yours did to me the other night I would think you would have wanted to steer clear of the jarhead," I replied, pushing him up against the wall. "You and those other fucking mugs had a grand old time with me the other night huh Dennis? You and them fucking dregs stripped me, fucking tied me up, shaved me to the goddamned skin and to top it all off you, YOU fucking milked me like I was a cow or something. That must have really gotten you your jollies huh? Making a marine cum like that over and over again? And not to mention it but I will anyway how you and your three perverted cronies had a great time finger fucking my damned bunghole. And fucking Howard, the blasted pervert, of all things, he steals my goddamned socks!"

"H-hey c'mon man, it was all just in fun," Dennis said pleadingly now, obviously realizing just how very pissed off I really was. "We're all friends' man; we were just having fun with you."

"I do not call what you and those three other faggots did to me fun Dennis!" I snarled at him. "But I'm not tired now *and* I am not tied up either!"

"But you will be," Dennis said with a smirk and tweaked the perfect knot in my necktie.

That was all I had to hear. I made a fist and was prepared to slam it into his face to wipe that smirk off it.

"Geoff, wait," Dennis suddenly rasped.

I hesitated for a microsecond and I was grabbed from behind. Dennis' three buddies had been there the whole fucking time just waiting for me to have my back turned to them. I had been tricked again!

"UHHHFFFFF!!!" I roared in stupefaction as they pulled me off him by my upper arms. "WH-what the fuck???"

"Got you," Dennis said snidely, pecked me on the cheek and tugged again at my necktie, a mean looking grin on his face. "Got you again. Did you honestly think I would be here alone, knowing you would be coming by? Fuck man, the marines did a good fucking job on your body Jarhead, but you still have a lot to learn when it comes to common sense."

"Damn it Dennis, damn all of you," I snarled as they yanked my arms up painfully behind my back and held them there.

I struggled like a crazed man in their grasps but it was no use. The fucking tricksters had me cold.

"Now, one more shave for the jarhead before he heads back to his base?" Dennis asked me, cupping my balls in his hand through my uniform pants. "And just for fun we'll blindfold him this time and for even more fun we'll see how many loads we can squeeze out of him today."

Dennis then jiggled my nuts in my uniform pants.

"D-Dennis, no, NO, not again man!!" I roared and struggled even more.

Dennis saw that I was not as dog-tired as I was when they had gotten the snag on me at two in the morning.

"Hate to have to do this to you buddy, but you need to calm down,"

Dennis said and squeezed my balls hard.

"AAAAYYYYY!!! OH GAWD!!" I groaned and the pain searing through me somewhat abated my struggles.

"Take him to the chair," Dennis said to his buddies.

Alex, Ronald and Howard hoisted me up off the floor by my upper arms and carried me to the spare room.

"NO, NO, oh Gawd, *no!!*" I snarled at them.

As we entered the room I saw the chair and all the shaving equipment set out and ready. GOD, they had planned this again! And I had stupidly walked right into their trap. From outside the room Dennis was laughing hysterically. Within a few minutes the fucking pranksters had me stripped down to my black calf length dress socks, sitting all spread out in the chair, tied tight blindfolded as well this time… Howard pushed my socks down to my ankles, telling me that they were his after they were done. I whimpered and seethed as they picked up the electric clipper razors and the sounds of buzzing filled the room…

MISSING IN ACTION

Author's note: The following story, "Missing in Action", I had originally written in the form of a play, which means I wrote this many years ago. Writing stories in the forms of plays was my original idea when it came to writing all that time ago. I found that it gave my character's their voices and it allowed me to add the third person dialogue/detail in as well, without having to actually write in the third person. As time went on I started writing a lot in the first person and then finally it was my novella length story "The Taming of Dominick" that I wrote in the third person. For my book of erotic military fetish stories I have decided to give "Missing in Action" a new spin and to tell it in the third person... Happy Reading from *Christopher Trevor*

Morning, it was 6:00 AM to be exact and United States army sergeant's Andre and Williams were standing side by side under a tree in the woods as their platoons of privates struggled through their basic training routines and intense exercises out on the nearby field. The two muscular, well-toned and well-built soldiers were clad in their olive colored fatigues complete with tall highly shined black combat boots that climbed to just under their knees.

"I tell you Williams, I can remember like it was yesterday when I was being put through basic training," Sergeant Andre, five feet nine, hugely muscular and well-toned, dark haired and with piercing dark eyes said to his buddy. "Fucking sweating it out, grunting and farting like these poor saps are now. Fuck, but this was a great idea you had today to pit your platoon against mine to compete in physical training drills."

"HA, that sounds pretty mean," Sergeant Williams, a soldier nearly six feet tall, built like a brick shit-house, with brown crew-cut hair and chestnut colored eyes replied, eyeing their troops as he spoke. "But tell me Andre, if you had to do it all over again, would you?"

"Sure as fuck man, I mean, look at me, sergeant at age thirty," Sergeant Andre replied. "I'll make general before you know it. There's nothing I can't handle and no goddamned obstacle I can't get over, just like on the course here, HA! And when I do make general the first thing I plan to do is have you in the gym doing push-ups in your underpants and goddamned combat boots for me while I whip your big hairy ass with my riding crop Williams, DOUBLE HA!!"

"Fuck you, you pervert, I always knew you had a thing or two for my big ass," Sergeant Williams responded laughingly.

"See if I'm kidding bud, after all the fucked up jokes you've pulled on me it'll be the least I can do to repay you," Sergeant Andre retorted and the two sergeants then directed their attention to their platoon detail.

Two hours later physical training was finished and the two sergeants's lined up their exhausted and sweaty charges for the trek back to the base.

"Listen Williams, do me a favor huh?" Sergeant Andre asked. "Take my platoon with yours back to the base. I have to go and take a nasty piss. I think I'll water the bushes a bit. I'll catch up with you later."

"Sure thing," Sergeant Williams said. "See you later..."

Sergeant Andre watched as his male and female platoon of privates headed back toward the base, them being led by his best buddy ever. Then, with a piss hard-on in his fatigue pants he trotted quickly into the woods to relieve himself. The handsomely rugged sergeant found a large tree, stood facing it, opened his fly and whipped out his huge hose-like cock. Women he had dated said that his cock was a handful. Other women he dated claimed it was beyond a mouthful. Sergeant Andre recalled once showing one of his female conquests that his cock more than filled her pussy. What was her name again the sergeant tried to recall as he prepared to piss on the ground in the woods? He chuckled meanly as he recalled the way whatever her name was panted and cried as he fucked her hard and deep with his gargantuan manhood. Sergeant

Andre was proud of his huge tube-steak like cock. And when he had to piss it was always erect like a flagpole. He spread his muscular legs and pissed hard, yellow and frothy against the tree.

"AAHHHHHH, better, better," the sergeant gurgled throatily as he pissed and pissed.

Relief filled the soldier as his bladder emptied and the last droplets of his piss splattered on the ground.

"Oh yeah, sometimes a good piss is better than a good cum," Sergeant Andre grunted with a sinister looking grin on his face.

Suddenly though, as he was about to tuck his enormous cock back into his fatigue pants a heavy duty rope that had been fashioned into a lasso fell around his muscular upper arms. The rope was quickly pulled tight and Sergeant Andre's arms were pinned to his chest and upper torso.

"H-HEY!!! WHAT the fuck?!?" the sergeant roared and whirled around, his cock still dangling embarrassingly out of his pants.

He expected to see Sergeant Williams standing there behind him, God knew he and his good buddy always played mean jokes on each other. It had become a sort of ritual between the two men since they had known each other. Instead he saw a bearded well-muscled man clad in work boots, jeans and a flannel shirt standing there holding the slack of the heavy-duty rope. Sergeant Andre guessed the man's age to be in the mid thirties to early forties. The man smiled mockingly at the army sergeant.

"Sergeant, don't you know that it's against the law to piss in the woods?"

As he spoke the man tugged hard on the rope, tightening it around the sergeant's arms and torso.

"Who the fuck are you?!?" Sergeant Andre demanded. "Release me now Mister!!"

But rather than release the soldier the man yanked Sergeant Andre over to him till they were face to face, the soldier's exposed cock swinging in the wind. Andre struggled madly but helplessly as he became more and more tangled up in the rope and then the man proceeded to tie the rope tightly around and around his upper arms, binding the soldier tighter yet.

A Boner Book

"FUCKING guy, what the hell is this all about?!?" Sergeant Andre bellowed. "HELP!! HELP!! SOMEONE HELP ME!!!"

"You may yell all you want Sergeant," the man chuckled as he tied his prey. "Your friend Sergeant Williams and both platoons have all gone back to the base. We are the only ones here now."

As the man spoke he tied and tied the rest of the rope around Sergeant Andre's arms, his upper body and knotted it securely around his neck, but not too secure so he did not cut off the soldier's circulation.

"Fuck, I demand an explanation Mister!!" Sergeant Andre seethed in his captor's face. "I am a United States army officer and what you're doing is a federal offense!"

Without a word the man squatted down in front of the bound up soldier and slurped his dangling, huge flaccid cock into his mouth. He instantly played "Suck" with Sergeant Andre's skin flute.

"OH SHIT, HOLY FUCKING SHIT!! You pervert!!" the captured sergeant roared in a mixture of ecstasy and pure rage. "YOU fucking degenerate! Leave my goddamned cock alone man!! That tube steak is for the ladies only!! AAAAHHRRRR SHIT!!!"

But even through his anger the soldier found himself growing hard and stiff in the man's mouth as he was expertly sucked on. He grunted breathlessly and was about to shoot a soldier-sized load of slop.

"You goddamned mother-fucker!!" Andre ranted as the man squeezed his big dangling balls a few times as he went on sucking.

Sergeant Andre's balls were the size of two kiwis in his sac and they were always super-sensitive to the touch. The soldier knew that the slightest contact with them from another could have him spurting uncontrollably.

"OH MY GOD, I'm going to cum Mister, you're going to make me shoot my goddamned load like fucking crazy!!!" the sergeant bellowed breathlessly.

Sergeant Andre watched as the man quickly took his mammoth-sized cock out of his mouth and grabbed it tightly in hand. The trapped sergeant swiveled his hips, rocked back a bit on his combat-booted feet and shot his load of GI slime in gushes all over the ground.

"OHHHHHHHH!!!! DAMN, OHHHHHH!!!" the soldier cried out loudly. "First I watered the bushes with my piss now I'm nourishing them with my soldier slop!! FUCKER!!!"

The man who had so easily captured the soldier stood up and faced his captive.

"Sergeant, my name is Alvin," the man said with a maniacal looking grin. "You and I are going to have lots of fun together."

"I-I don't understand," Sergeant Andre said, still breathless from having shot his load just moments ago, still mortified at the fact that his now spent cock was still dangling out of his fatigues pants.

"Earlier I heard you say that you could conquer any obstacle," Alvin said to the captured soldier, giving his sensitive and sexy feeling cock a tug or two, getting a good breathless sigh from his captive. "Well, I'm an obstacle, a huge obstacle. I hereby challenge you to conquer me."

"*Conquer you?*" Sergeant Andre prattled. "When I'm all tied up like this? Man, you are fucking crazy! And where were you spying on me and buddy Sergeant Williams that you heard me say that? Fucking guy man, you're some kind of psychotic nut-job!!"

Suddenly, Sergeant Andre turned on his heels and began running away from the man named Alvin.

"Run if you want Sergeant Andre, run all you want!" the bound soldier heard the man shouting from behind him. "You won't get far, that I promise!!"

"If I can get to the road maybe I can hail a car and get some help," Sergeant Andre said to himself.

As he ran the sergeant tried to untie himself but quickly found out that the ropes were tied too tight. He then looked down at his still exposed cock.

"Damn, that son of a bitch sucked my cock *and* got me off!" he went on thinking miserably. "How in the hell am I going to hail a car with my beefy cock sticking out of my goddamned pants?!?"

When Sergeant Andre reached the road he saw a car and figured he would just have to take his chances. He began (ridiculously looking) jumping up and down in the road, his slimy cock bouncing up and down and the oncoming car came to a slow halt.

"Thank God," Sergeant Andre said loudly. "Please help me!!"

Without thinking the sergeant ran to the driver's side of the car, leaned down, looked in the car window and saw…

"May I be of assistance Sergeant?" Alvin asked his handsome captive.

"SHIT!!!" Sergeant Andre grunted and Alvin stepped quickly out of the car, the soldier slowly backing away from him, realizing that running was futile.

"Look, Mister, I don't know what the fuck you want...but..." Sergeant Andre began.

"I've already told you what I want Sergeant, now, *get in the car,*" Alvin said sternly.

"What?!? Fuck man, but that's kidnapping!!" Sergeant Andre said fearfully as Alvin grabbed his arm.

He marched the captured soldier around the car and forced him into the passenger seat of the car.

"After your little runaway stunt you're lucky I'm not making you ride in the trunk Sergeant Andre," Alvin said and slammed the passenger seat door closed.

"Fuck, this is unbelievable," Sergeant Andre said miserably. "WH-where the fuck are you taking me Mister?"

"Home Sergeant, I'm taking you home," Alvin said and started the car.

Alvin drove for about ten minutes and pulled up in front of a lone house which was situated on the edge of the woods.

"This is where you live?" Sergeant Andre asked, looking at the house.

All Alvin said in response was "Yes" and stepped out of the car. He walked around to the passenger side of the vehicle and opened the door. Still helplessly bound Sergeant Andre stepped out of the car and took in the sight of the small lonely looking house.

"Y-you live here all alone?" the sergeant asked, wondering if this man named Alvin had other surprises tucked away in the house.

Once more all Alvin said was, "Yes."

"God, it looks all rundown," Sergeant Andre said to himself. "What the fuck is this guy's story???" Holding Sergeant Andre by one arm Alvin led his captive up the steps and into the house. He locked the door behind them and the soldier looked around at the worn furniture, the old scraggly looking rugs and the peeling paint on the walls.

"Fuck, but how can he live here?!?" Sergeant Andre asked himself, he being a solider used to meticulousness, cleanliness and order.

But then, the sergeant noticed a picture of a young man dressed in a formal army uniform hanging on one of the walls. He disengaged himself from Alvin's grip on his arm and walked slowly over to where the picture hung for a closer look.

"Is this you Mister?" Sergeant Andre asked and Alvin said "Yes", sounding almost broken-hearted.

"You served?" the sergeant asked next.

"For a short time I did, yes," Alvin said, stepping next to the tied up soldier.

"Uh, why a short time?" Sergeant Andre asked next.

"I suppose you might say I was dishonorably discharged,' Alvin replied.

"Can I ask why?" the sergeant asked.

"My sergeant caught me having sex with one of the other men," Alvin said and Sergeant Andre turned and looked at his captor. From the way his home looked it was hard to believe that this man had ever been a soldier.

"So is that why you've kidnapped me?" Sergeant Andre asked incredulously, although now seeing from a psychological point of view where all this was headed. "Are you planning on getting even with your sergeant through me?"

Alvin smiled fiendishly and said, "Not exactly" and cupped his captive's chin in his hand.

"You see Sergeant Andre, I got even with him a long time ago," Alvin snickered.

"H-how?" Sergeant Andre asked, although somehow he already knew the answer to that question.

"I killed him," Alvin replied and Sergeant Andre gulped hard.

"Come with me," Alvin said and brought his prisoner to his kitchen where he quickly got him stretched out on a long wooden table on his back.

"WH-what are you going to do man?" Sergeant Andre asked fearfully. "Look, I'm not the sergeant who had you dishonorably discharged okay?"

"Just take it easy Sergeant Andre," Alvin said.

Without another word Alvin leaned down and slurped Sergeant Andre's semi-erect cock into his mouth for a second time.

"OH NO!! NO!!! Not again man!" Sergeant Andre seethed, lifting his head up off the table. "PLEASE stop, I'm still all sensitive and sexy feeling from before…"

Ignoring the sergeant's rants Alvin trailed his tongue over and over Andre's cock in his mouth, teasing it, getting it hard. Like women who had sucked his meat pole Sergeant Andre saw how his hugeness filled Alvin's mouth. The guy's jaws were puffed out nearly to the breaking point as he sucked the soldier's cock.

"I have got to get away from this guy!" Sergeant Andre said to himself. "But I'm all tied up!! What the fuck am I going to do?!?"

Then, as his cock was being sucked for the second time that day Sergeant Andre came up with an idea…

"Wait, my arms are tied, but my feet aren't," he thought as a feeling of impending victory coursed through his being.

With that, Sergeant Andre raised one knee and slammed it as hard as possible into Alvin's head.

"UFFFFF!!!" was the sound that Alvin made as Sergeant Andre's cock slipped from his mouth and he fell to his knees, only dazed though…

Sergeant Andre quickly sat up and kicked Alvin hard in the head with the toe-section of one of his combat booted feet.

"ARRGHHH!!!" Alvin cried out in pain and this time fell to the floor.

The still bound up sergeant hopped down off the table.

"You sick bastard!!" Sergeant Andre bellowed and stepped over Alvin.   He ran to the entrance of the house.

"DAMN it!!" the soldier seethed through clenched teeth. "How am I going to open the fucking door roped up like this???"

Thinking fast, the well-muscled soldier pressed himself up against the door and managed to get a hand around the knob. He turned the small lock and then pushed the door open.

"Did it!!" he rejoiced and ran out of the house and down the short flight of steps.

"I'll have to go through the woods to get back to the base," Andre said as he ran as fast as possible.

But as the bound up soldier passed a huge tree his foot tripped a thin wire. He was suddenly scooped up by a booby-trap net and abruptly found himself hanging from a branch on the tree.

"SHIT, SHIT, SHIT!!!!" Sergeant Andre ranted fearfully and angrily. "GOD DAMN IT all!!"

He looked over at the house and saw Alvin coming out of the front door carrying a rifle. As if he had not been clocked twice on the head Alvin walked calmly over to Sergeant Andre. The sergeant wondered if his captor had a head of steel.

"I must say Sergeant Andre, you are a very resourceful man, a soldier of the highest caliber," Alvin said. "But I'm through playing this cat and mouse game with you. I didn't abduct you so that I could keep chasing you through the woods.

"NO?!?" Andre sputtered. "Why did you abduct me??? So that you could keep sucking my goddamned cock???"

Alvin raised his rifle.

"NO!! OH NO!!" Andre suddenly pleaded. "Don't kill me man!! Please, don't fucking kill me! What did I ever do to you???"

Alvin aimed and shot the rope holding the net. Andre fell to the ground.

"OOOOFFFFF!!!" the soldier grunted as he landed in a netted heap.

Moments later Sergeant Andre was standing before Alvin with his uniform pants off and his feet tied. The soldier now wore his black spit-shined combat boots, thick olive colored army issued sweat socks, white briefs with his sausage-sized cock sticking out of them and the top portion of his fatigues uniform. As he stood there feeling totally helpless Alvin stepped behind him and tied a blindfold over the soldier's eyes.

"*Shit, shit, shit...*" Sergeant Andre panted miserably.

When Alvin was done tying the white cloth blindfold over the sergeant's eyes he gently squeezed his ass.

"Why are you doing this to me man???" the sergeant asked, sounding desperate and terrified at that point. I never did anything to you! Fuck, I don't even know you Mister!"

"Tell me Sergeant, if I were a woman, would you mind this so much?"

"Being kidnapped?" Andre replied in question. "Sure I would mind…"

"Imagine you're a P.O.W. Sergeant Andre," Alvin chuckled and squeezed Andre's ass again. "The army teaches you how to deal with being taken prisoner, if it were to happen that is."

"Oh sure, but if I were a P.O.W. my captors would be after vital top secret information, not my cock!" Sergeant Andre retorted. "And please stop squeezing my goddamned ass you pervert!"

Then, Alvin squatted down in front of the sergeant and once more slurped his cock into his mouth.

"UHHHHH, damn you man!!" the bound and blindfolded soldier panted.

Alvin expertly sucked Sergeant Andre to a full hard-on, slapping his thighs a few times.

"OHHHHHHHH…" Sergeant Andre gasped. "UHHHHHH… fucking guy just loves my goddamned cock…"

Like earlier Alvin squeezed the sergeant's balls as he sucked his cock.

"OH GOD, oh God man, I'm going to shoot my load of slop again!" Andre panted. "OHHHHH JEEZ man, my goddamned balls are so fucking sensitive…"

Alvin quickly took Sergeant Andre's cock out of his mouth and grabbed it in hand. The sergeant shot his load, squirting it like a hose all over the ground, grunting and gurgling as he did. When he was done his body relaxed and Alvin stood up.

"Fuck, I will say this for you Mister, you give damn good head," Sergeant Andre huffed.

"I knew you would start seeing things my way Sergeant," Andre said.

"Oh yeah?" Andre asked. "How about taking off this blindfold so I can see a lot more things?"

"Not just yet Sergeant, not just yet," was Alvin's reply.

A few moments later Alvin was walking back to his house, his rifle slung over one shoulder, his prisoner slung over the other.

"Man, I am in a SHIT-load of trouble here," Sergeant Andre said to himself as he was carried like a sack of laundry. "I sure hope Williams realizes that I'm not back and sends out a search patrol...or something..."

But, as Sergeant Andre was carried helplessly back to Alvin's house Sergeant Williams was at that same moment in his private office. Clad now in his dress uniform the burly and rugged sergeant had other things besides Sergeant Andre on his mind when he heard the knock at his door.

"Yeah, come on in," Sergeant Williams called out, sounding as brusque as possible.

Two privates stepped into the office, closing and locking the door behind them. They looked across the room at their sergeant, saluted and stood instantly and rigidly at attention.

"You sent for us Sir?" the first private asked, a young well-built twenty year old blond guy from Nebraska.

"I sure as shit did guys," Sergeant Williams replied with a sly looking grin on his face as he took a pair of handcuffs and a blindfold out of the top drawer of his desk. "Okay you guys, strip down. I think you should know this routine by now."

The two privates shouted out a hearty "Yes Sir!!!" in unison and quickly stripped out of their uniforms. When they were naked the first private said, "Now it's your turn Sergeant Williams, Sir." Within a few scant minutes the horned up Sergeant Williams was nude except for his black calf length dress socks. The burly sergeant's fat cock stuck out hard in front of him, almost as if it were pledging allegiance to the two privates. The two privates locked Sergeant Williams' hands behind him in his own handcuffs and blindfolded him. The sergeant spread his legs wide and stood balanced before his two underlings. The two privates then proceeded to run their hands over the sergeant's huge rock-hard chest and they squeezed and teased his colossal-sized fat nipples.

"Out on the field you may be in charge Sergeant Williams Sir, but in here *we are*," the second private, a lanky, five foot nine brown haired, brown eyed twenty something year old kid from down south chuckled as he tugged on the sergeant's earlobe.

Sergeant Williams smiled behind his blindfold and the two privates took a suck each on his bulbous nipples, flicking their tongues over the pointed tips of them.

"Get busy you two," Sergeant Williams suddenly barked.

The first private knelt behind the handcuffed and blindfolded sergeant, spread his ass globes wide apart and began lapping and licking his hole, slurping the sergeant's ass chowder greedily down his throat. The second private sucked heartily at the sergeant's nipples, working them alternately.

"OOOOOHHHHH yeah, fucking A you mugs," Sergeant Williams panted. "All I could think about today out on the physical training field was having you two in here eating my mangy ass, servicing my goddamned tits and then playing FUCK with you guys!"

The sergeant's cock grew harder in seconds. The first private slapped Williams' hard ass globes a few times while his face was buried in his crack.

"MMMMMM oh yeah, lick my hole, suck my tits!!" Sergeant Williams demanded. "FUCK YEAH!!!" As the two privates worked him over Sergeant Williams' cock grew as hard as steel, his balls hung down low like two lemons in his hairy sac...

The second private then leaned over the desk and spread his legs apart. The first private guided the blindfolded sergeant behind him.

"Okay Sergeant Williams Sir, his ass is right in front of you," the first private said, squeezing his sergeant's rock-hard ass globes, loving the feel of them.

Williams pushed his cock into the second private's ass slowly, the tip of his cock kissing the kid's rosebud and then he plowed in up to his balls, fucking the private's most clandestine crevice.

"OH YEAH!!" the second private gasped at the invasion. "Fuck me Sir; fuck me with that gargantuan cock!! OH YEAH!"

As Sergeant Williams fucked the second private the first private continued licking and lapping at the sergeant's asshole. "OHHHHRR fuck yeah!!" Sergeant Williams croaked throatily.

It went on and on like that for a while, Sergeant Williams pounding hard on the second private's ass with his big cock wedged deep inside the kid while the first private feverishly drooled in the burly sergeant's ass and slurped it back out again, driving the handcuffed and blindfolded sergeant stir-crazy.

"Oh yeah, going to fill your hot ass with my soldier-sized load of cum!!" Sergeant Williams grunted. "Oh yeah!!"

Sergeant Williams shot his hefty load and the second private felt the soldier's warm thick creamy fluid fill his hole.

"OH YEAH, FUCK YEAH, Yes Sir Sergeant Williams Sir!" the second private gasped and panted as Sergeant Williams thrust like crazy inside him, him grunting like a real soldier.

Next, the two privates sat Sergeant Williams up on his desk. The spent sergeant took heavy breaths as his two underlings began licking one of his big feet each and jacking themselves off at the same time. Sergeant Williams was still handcuffed and blindfolded.

"OH YEAH, fucking A, lick my stinking feet!" Sergeant Williams snorted. "Suck my smelly socks!"

Within a few minutes the sergeant's black socks were soaked with saliva, then, the first private removed the sergeant's blindfold and Williams watched as the two privates shot their loads all over his black socked feet.

"Damn, no one on this base has it better than me," Sergeant Williams said to himself behind a fiendish looking grin. "Look at these two, licking my feet like two obedient puppies!"

A short while later the three men were dressed. The two privates left Sergeant Williams' office and Williams put the handcuffs and blindfold back in his desk, a smile of true contentment on his handsome face...

As for Sergeant Andre Alvin now had him in an upstairs room in his house, the sergeant securely tied to a chair. Sergeant Andre had by then been completely stripped of his fatigues uniform. He wore only his socks and a gag. His blindfold was dangling around his neck. He watched as Alvin knelt before him, sucking his balls, tongue lapping them, polishing them, bathing them in his mouth. The bound up sergeant's huge cock pointed straight up at the ceiling, long, beefy and hard.

"Damn, if he keeps treating my balls the way he's doing they're going to be swollen to the size of tennis balls," Sergeant Andre thought. "MMMMMFFF..."

Alvin simply ignored the sounds Sergeant Andre made behind his gag and continued sucking/torturing his testicles.

"OH DAMN, I'm going to cum again!!" the sergeant said to himself. "MMMMFFFF!!!"

Then, Sergeant Andre did indeed shoot his load, squirting it all over his chest… Alvin looked up mockingly at his prisoner.

"I must say, you cum like a sergeant, over and over again," Alvin snickered. "And that time I wasn't stroking or sucking your cock." Filled with mortification Sergeant Andre looked away from the man who had so expertly captured him. Alvin stood up, stepped behind Sergeant Andre and tied the blindfold back over his eyes.

"I'll be back soon, give you some time to boil up some more soup for me," Alvin said, his hand on the back of the sergeant's neck as he spoke. "Next time I'm going to eat your cum…"

Sergeant Andre heard Alvin leave the room, closing the door behind him.

"Oh God Williams, please do something…I need help here!" Sergeant Andre thought miserably. "I'm being milked like a roped steer…"

That afternoon, while Sergeant Andre sat tied to a chair, Sergeant Williams was just getting back to his office after having lunch with a few of his buddies on the base. He walked into his office and was surprised to see the second private from earlier sitting behind his desk.

"Well, well, and look who's sitting at my desk," Sergeant Williams said with a smirk, walking slowly over to the handsome boyish looking soldier. "Can I help you Private?"

The private instantly jumped to his feet, saluted and stood at attention before the burly sergeant, his lips close enough to kiss Williams'.

"I hope so Sir, I truly do hope so," the private said heartily, his cock hard as a rock in his khaki pants. "But Sergeant Williams Sir, we'll need the handcuffs and blindfold…"

Sergeant Williams smiled meanly. He had these two right where he wanted them. All they wanted to do was service him it seemed, and he was just too happy to oblige…

A few short minutes later Sergeant Williams was stripped to his black socks, handcuffed and blindfolded. His cock was instantly rigid and stiff as the private began by kissing his nipples, sucking them, pinching them and then working his tongue down to his stomach, licking him all over.

"OH YEAH fucks yeah, twice in one day, lick me man," Sergeant Williams huffed. "Fucking lick me you horny bastard…"

"UMMMMM!!" the private responded and Williams' jaw dropped when he heard the private say, "Going to fuck you Sergeant Williams Sir."

"No way boy, no fucking way," Sergeant Williams replied. "Nobody fucks me!"

"You fucked me earlier," the private said in between kissing the sergeant's stomach area.

"That's right kid," Sergeant Williams went on. "But like I said, no one but no one fucks me!"

The private stopped licking the sergeant, stood up straight and looked at him, his gaze almost penetrating. Even blindfolded the sergeant could feel the private's stare. Somehow Sergeant Williams knew he had gotten himself into some trouble this time. He knew that by feeding his fetish of vulnerability by letting himself be handcuffed and blindfolded he was always taking a chance. But none of the privates that serviced him ever turned on him…until now it seemed.

"Sir, you really aren't in a position to try to stop me," the private said.

Williams licked his lips nervously as the private took him by his upper arms and proceeded to slump him over his desk.

"N-now look Private, I want you to stop this!" Sergeant Williams said sternly.

"And what will you do if I don't?" the private asked teasingly. "Bring me up on charges perhaps?"

Sergeant Williams felt panicked as the private roughly yanked his legs apart as wide as possible.

"Now hold still while I get naked you handsome fuck," the private said.

"NOW look, get me up on my desk and start licking my goddamned stinking feet and servicing my socks!" Sergeant Williams grunted. "That's an order Private!"

But the private ignored him and moments later he was completely undressed. He stepped behind Williams and placed his hands on the sergeant's hips. Sergeant Williams felt the private's hard-on rubbing against his ass.

"Holy shit man..." Williams seethed and the private slapped his ass twice.

"I take it this will be the first time someone ever fucked your mangy ass huh Sarge?" the private asked his commanding officer in a mocking tone of voice and slapped Williams' ass again.

"Y-yes, it will be, unless you decide to do the right thing and change your mind," Sergeant Williams said, sounding desperate now.

In response to his sergeant's request the private plunged his hard-on into Williams' hole.

"AAAARRRRR!!!" Sergeant Williams seethed loudly.

"MMM...the sound of the cherry popping," the private mused.

As Williams was fucked hard Sergeant Andre heard the door to the room he was in opening. Alvin walked back in...

"I'm back Sergeant," Alvin said. "Have you been producing more cum for me?"

"What I've been doing is working on getting loose from these ropes," Sergeant Andre said to himself. "A little more and my hands will be free!"

Alvin removed the sergeant's blindfold and kneeled down in front of him. He instantly slurped the soldier's cock into his mouth and began sucking it.

"MMMFFFF..." Sergeant Andre sputtered and said to himself, "When I'm free I'm going to give you a beating you will never forget Mister!"

The sergeant managed to finally free his hands. He made a ham-sized fist and brought it down hard atop Alvin's head.

"UNNNN!!!" Alvin gasped in shock and fell to the floor in front of the sergeant, Andre's cock sliding out of his mouth.

The sergeant quickly pulled the gag out of his mouth and reached down to untie his feet.

"I swear to God and all the angels in heaven Mister, YOU'VE HAD IT!!" Sergeant Andre seethed. "When I get through with you you'll wish you'd never been born!"

As Sergeant Andre worked at untying himself Alvin squirmed on the floor and moaned awfully. Then, he lifted his head and as his vision cleared a bit he saw the soldier undoing the knots in the ropes that had been holding him to the chair. As Alvin looked upward he watched as the soldier stood up and loomed menacingly over him.

"Now, get on your feet Mister!!" Sergeant Andre roared.

But instead, Alvin, in a lightning like motion grabbed Sergeant Andre's ankles and pulled hard, toppling the soldier. Andre fell backwards over the chair and landed hard on his back.

"UHHHFFF!!!" the sergeant grunted.

"You should have hit me harder Sergeant!" Alvin said as he scrambled to his feet, reached down and once more grabbed Andre's ankles.

"You are in real trouble now Sergeant!" Alvin said as Andre tried to pull out of his grasp.

Instead the soldier found himself being dragged toward the stairs.

"Damn you man!!! GOD DAMN YOU!!" Sergeant Andre roared. "Let go of my feet!!"

The enraged soldier pounded the floor with his meaty fists as Alvin dragged him toward the stairs.

"I had hoped that I wouldn't have to take you to the basement Sergeant," Alvin said. "But you've left me no choice it would seem…"

Then, Alvin quickly faced forward with Sergeant Andre's ankles under his arms. He started down the stairs, dragging the soldier helplessly along with him on his ass. Sergeant Andre quickly placed his hands over his head as he was pulled down the stairs.

"UFFFFFFF!!!" the sergeant grunted. "You sick bastard!!"

When they reached the bottom of the stairs Alvin dragged his prisoner through the main floor and toward the basement steps. The sergeant saw his uniform fatigues on the couch.

"Jeez," the solider said miserably.

Once more he placed his hands over his head as he was meanly dragged down the basement steps.

"UUUHHHNNNNN!!!" Sergeant Andre seethed. "My ass is going to be all bruised Mister!!"

When they reached the bottom of the stairs the sergeant looked around and his eyes opened wide in disbelief.

"SHIT, SHIT, SHIT!!!" the soldier bellowed and was helplessly dragged around the basement by Alvin.

As Sergeant Andre struggled fruitlessly in his captor's strong grasp Sergeant Williams was also in trouble, although by definition of the word "trouble" he was not in as hot water as Sergeant Andre currently was. The private had just finished fucking Williams' no longer virgin ass, having filled the handcuffed and blindfolded sergeant's hole to the rim with his cum. The private now had Sergeant Williams propped against a wall. Sergeant Williams stood rigidly still as the private tied an elastic string around and around his balls. Sergeant Williams was still handcuffed and blindfolded. His cock throbbed long and hard, pointing straight up at the ceiling. Actually, the sergeant was at the moment of the belief that his cock was "fear hard."

"You will pay for this you know, Private," Sergeant Williams seethed, the feeling of his balls being tied driving him crazy.

"Maybe I will Sir, but for now it's worth it," the private responded mockingly.

The private finished binding the sergeant's balls. He then walked Williams over to his desk and laid him across it on his stomach.

"You wanted your feet licked huh?" the private asked. "Okay, I suppose you've sweated in those socks long enough. When I'm done licking them I'm going to shove those socks of yours in your mouth... SIR!!"

"Damn you Private!" Sergeant Williams grunted as his underling lifted his feet into the air and began licking and slobbering over the bottoms of them.

"MMMM..." the private crooned and Sergeant Williams' fear hard cock and bound balls throbbed under him.

The private sucked Sergeant Williams' toes through his thin black socks and caressed his iron-like calves.

"OH fuck yeah," Sergeant Williams panted.

"Can't deny that you're enjoying this eh Sir?" the private asked tauntingly.

"We'll talk when this is over Private," Sergeant Williams replied. "Believe me boy, WE WILL TALK!!"

"Of course Sir, but you won't be doing much talking when I cram these soggy socks of yours in your mouth," the private said.

The private then stopped servicing his sergeant's feet. He proceeded to roll the first black sock off Williams' left foot, bunching it up into a tight ball. He then took the second one off the sergeant's right foot but did not roll that sock up. Then, the private stepped in front of his blindfolded and handcuffed superior officer.

"Open wide Sergeant Williams, Sir!" the private commanded, the two men's roles having obviously been reversed.

"DAMN IT, damn you!!" Sergeant Williams prattled angrily and left with no choice but to do as he was being told he opened his mouth wide.

Smiling evilly the private crammed the sergeant's rolled up sock into his mouth and used the other one to tie it securely in place.

"RRRMMMFFF!!!" Sergeant Williams gurgled.

"Yes Sir, if you say so," the private laughed. "Damn, it's a shitty thing to do to a guy when you gag him with his stinking socks, HA!!"

While Sergeant Williams was sucking his stinking socks and chewing on them Sergeant Andre was now stretched out on his back on a long sturdy wooden table down in Alvin's basement. The sergeant was tied in a spread eagle position atop the table and watched helplessly as Alvin played suck with his cock and toyed with his balls.

"MMM...going to eat your cum this time Sergeant," Alvin said in between sucking.

"Damn it all," Sergeant Andre said to himself. "How does this nut keep getting over on me? The next time I get myself untied I cannot let him capture me again!" As his cock was sucked the bound soldier looked around the basement. On the walls he saw whips of various sizes and styles hanging from clips and hooks. On shelves he saw handcuffs, gags of various styles and blindfolds.

"Jeez, what kind of person is he?" Sergeant Andre asked himself.

But then, the soldier's thoughts were cut off when he felt himself shooting his load.

"OHHHRRRR YEAH, fuck, FUCK, I'm shooting my damned load again!!" the sergeant panted.

And, true to his word Alvin chugged down and swallowed every drop of Sergeant's Andre's homemade milkshake.

"MMM, you're delicious Sergeant Andre," Alvin said.

"Now will you let me go??" the soldier demanded.

"Not just yet Sergeant, not just yet," Alvin snickered.

Sergeant Andre watched as Alvin picked up something from a shelf. The soldier gulped hard when he saw what it was…

Moments later Sergeant Andre was standing with his hands tied tightly behind him and his feet tied together as well. Alvin placed a leather hood (with attached blindfold and dildo shaped gag) over Sergeant Andre's head, leaving his mouth and eyes uncovered…for the moment.

"What the fuck now man???" Sergeant Andre asked fearfully.

"I have a proposition for you Sergeant," Alvin replied.

"I'm listening," the sergeant responded.

"If you can get upstairs and put on your uniform while wearing this hood I'll let you go free," Alvin said.

"Oh yeah, what's the catch?" Sergeant Andre asked.

"You'll be blindfolded and gagged," Alvin said. "You'll have to find the uniform, put it on, and that includes properly lacing up your combat boots."

"And if I don't succeed?" Sergeant Andre inquired.

"Then you're mine Sergeant," Alvin said, sounding totally sinister.

Alvin covered Andre's eyes and gagged him with the hood attachments.

"Now, your uniform is in the living room upstairs," Alvin told Sergeant Andre. "Do you think you can get there?"

Andre nodded "Yes" most eagerly.

"Okay then, I'm going to untie your hands and feet," Alvin said. "But I warn you Sergeant Andre, any attempts to escape or to remove the hood will not be tolerated. Do you understand?"

Sergeant Andre again nodded "Yes" and Alvin proceeded to untie the soldier's hands and feet.

"And…go!!" Alvin quipped, as if the sergeant was running a race. "You have only ten minutes."

Sergeant Andre felt his way carefully over to the stairs. He stubbed his toe once as he began the ascent up the stairs, Alvin following behind him. Halfway up the sergeant stumbled and Alvin slapped his ass hard.

"RRRMMMFFF…" Sergeant Andre sputtered.

"Move it Sergeant!!" Alvin ordered. "Your time is precious!!"

Sergeant Andre reached the top of the stairs and pushed the basement door open. He carefully felt his way through the kitchen, running his hands along the table he had lain on earlier.

"If he would put some distance between us I would have time to uncover my eyes and finally take him," the sergeant said to himself.

But, miraculously Sergeant Andre found his way to the living room. He located his uniform on the couch.

"I did it!!" he thought triumphantly.

Sergeant Andre felt around on the couch first for his fatigue pants. He found them and quickly pulled them on. Next, he located his fatigue style tee shirt and pulled it on over his hooded head.

"Hurry Sergeant, your time is running out!" he heard Alvin say.

Ignoring him Sergeant Andre dropped to his knees and felt around on the floor for his combat boots.

"Damn, they have to be around here somewhere," he mumbled.

With luck on his side the sergeant found his boots, pulled them on and thanks to intense training he laced them up, pulling his socks up as well. When he was done he stood up.

"I bet this fucker didn't realize how easy this would be for me," the sergeant thought.

"Time is up Sergeant," Alvin snickered as the soldier was adjusting his tee shirt about his neck.

"And so is yours FUCKER!!" Sergeant Andre seethed to himself, reached up and pulled the blindfold attachment on the hood away from his eyes.

As Alvin approached him Sergeant Andre pulled the gag out of his mouth, spitting as he did so to get the leathery taste from his buds.

"Gag and blindfold me huh Fucker??" Sergeant Andre bellowed loudly. "Suck a soldier's cock and steal his sperm huh??? COME ON MAN, I'm ready for you now!" As Alvin stormed at the sergeant in a rage Andre assumed a kickboxing position and landed three hard and unforgiving blows to Alvin's face, (he heard Alvin's nose break) stomach and finally his legs.

"UHHHFFFF!!!" Alvin sputtered, blood flying from his nose as he fell to the floor.

Sergeant Andre angrily took the hood off and flung it across the room.

"You will not get the drop on me again Alvin my man!!" Sergeant Andre roared, looking down at the unconscious man who had captured him.

"Fuck, I should kill you..." Sergeant Andre said the tip of his combat-booted foot scant inches from Alvin's bleeding nose.

But the sergeant managed to get his anger under control and he trudged out of the house...

Two hours later Sergeant Andre was back at the base.

He walked into Sergeant Williams' office and found his buddy sitting behind his desk.

"Hey Andre, where the fuck have you been all day?" Williams asked, his asshole still smarting. "That was one long piss you took."

"Williams, you would not believe it if I told you," Sergeant Andre said, still wondering if his buddy had planned his kidnap.

"Really?" Sergeant Williams asked. "You should hear about my day then." The two soldiers smiled at each other.

The Captain of the Football Team

"OHHHHHHHH GAWD, gggrrrrrmmmfffff!!!!" I sputtered as I swallowed yet another scoop of ice cream that was laced liberally with rum. "FUUUCCCHHH, OH FUUCCCHHHH, fucking lousy thing to be doing to the captain of the football team you miserable bastards!"

I was fed, or should I say force-fed another whopping sized scoop of the rum laced ice cream. The dairy treat was making my stomach doing flip-flops let me tell you. My poor stomach churned as I swallowed it as fast as possible. Fucking guys were force-feeding me faster than I could chug it down. And every time I swallowed there was more of the good stuff to be eaten.

"Not so lousy when said captain of said football team is the captain of the *opposing* college team Johnny boy, oh Johnny boy," Alex said cheerfully and yanked my head back by a handful of my brown wavy sweat soaked hair. "And you know that when it comes to college rivalries all is fair in football and war. More beer for the captain of the winning team!"

Alex shoved a funned in my mouth and his sinister buddy Ronald gleefully poured cold beer into it, forcing me to guzzle it down.

"GGGRRRRRMMMMFFF," I gasped as what I could not swallow of the beer seeped sloppily out of the sides of my funnel covered lips.

It dripped down over my bared muscular chest, mixing with the various flavors of rum-laced ice cream that I had not been able to swallow either. Damn, but I was a creamy and beery mess buds. I looked at Alex through anger-filled eyes as he held my head back.

"Having fun eh Johnny boy, oh Johnny boy?" he asked me mockingly and jiggled my head with the handful of my hair that he was holding.

"GRRRFFFFF…" I grunted as I chugged beer.

"You know, I wonder if the guys on the winning team have noticed at this point that they're missing their captain," Ronald said in a gloating tone of voice after having stopped pouring the beer in the funnel. "They were all so damned anxious to get back to their turf that they didn't realize that Johnny boy, oh Johnny boy here wasn't with them on either of their buses."

"Yeah, and we got him," Alex said laughingly, took the funnel out of my mouth and pushed my head forward.

"You fuckers!!" I shouted angrily through a beer slogged mouth and throat, but then Dennis was holding a metal scoop filled with vanilla rum-laced ice cream in front of my soaked and trembling lips.

He forced the ice cream into my mouth by slapping the scoop against my craw and I scoffed it down again. I made angry sputtering noises as I was again force-fed the dairy treat. GAWD, they had been at it now for nearly an hour and to be perfectly honest my head was spinning. DAMN, almost an hour since a few of the guys from the losing college football team had managed to snag me right out of the "visitors locker room" and lugged my sexy ass to Alex's dorm room. After I swallowed the ice cream Dennis squatted in front of me and took my semi hard (hard with anger mostly) cock that was sticking out of the fly opening of my boxer shorts in his hand.

"OHHHHHH GAWD, no, no, not again you pervert," I ranted as the guy stroked me up to a nice big beefy boy hard-on. "This is beyond mortifying, JEEZ!"

My cock was pudged and pulsing in the fucking guy's paw.

"Ha, that'll be the third fucking time that Johnny boy, oh Johnny boy shoots his load, if he cums that is," Ronald laughed, holding a fresh bottle of cold beer at the ready.

"Oh he'll cum, he'll cum, trust me on that, my hands are magic when it comes to getting a slob like Johnny boy, oh Johnny boy off," Dennis chuckled as he stroked me a tad faster.

Fucking bastards planned to get me better than sopping and

stinking drunk before sending me back to my college campus, totally humiliated…and being jacked off by a member of the opposing college team was humiliation defined to a tee buds. And in the position I was in there wasn't all that much I could do to stop them. You see, I was securely roped to a straight back wooden chair, my hands tied securely behind me, I was wearing just my white boxer shorts and white sweat socks pushed down around my ankles. Mounds of rope were wound over and over my upper muscular body, pinning me securely to the goddamned chair. I was ripe with the scent of sweat from the football game that I had recently led my team through and the scent of rum laced with ice cream and beer accumulating all over my upper body and stomach area. I looked like a real slob sitting there, the remnants of the ice cream and beer they had fed me that I could not swallow dripping from my chops and down onto my torso. My boxers were also soaked and pungently scented with the champagne that my teammates had sprayed and poured over me back in the locker room. And…to make my situation all the more worse Alex (fucking practical joker that he is) had jammed a big fat latex butt-plug into my asshole. I squirmed miserably under the ropes on that damned thing as my poor stomach churned and churned like a washing machine…and let's not forget that Dennis had my manhood in his hand at the moment.

"OHHHHHH FUCK, getting close again you fucker," I seethed at Dennis as he stroked and choked my cock faster. "You're goin' to get another hefty load of football player spunk out of me!!! AAARRRHHHH FUCK…"

As I grunted and swore toward shooting a third load for the practical jokers Ronald raised his eyebrows at me, grinning meanly. A feeling of utter dismay washed over me as he held that bottle of beer at the ready. At that point I had actually lost count of how many bottles of beer and scoops of rum laced ice cream I had been forced to consume. I only knew that when the time came I would be in the men's room for quite a while, really stinking the place up, HARDY HAR HAR, fuckers. That is if these guys decided to untie me anytime soon. Shit, I was suffering this horrible joke of jokes because my college team had won the football game, on the opposing team's turf no less. I could understand their anger. I could also understand their glee at getting the drop on and kidnapping the captain of the winning team. Sometimes the losing team would kidnap the winning team's mascot as a joke. Sometimes the losing team would go so far as to kidnap the player of the winning team who scored the winning touchdown. When the guy was returned to his teammates more times out of many his head had been shaved bald along with his eyebrows and so had his pubic area, HARDY HAR HAR again fuckers. In this case however, a few members of the losing team went after the winning team's captain, yours truly, hunky Johnny Richardson, nicknamed Johnny boy, oh Johnny boy, twenty-one year old super jock. And it was my own fault that they had nabbed my sorry and sexy ass. All because I was the last dude left in the visiting team's locker room. Totally winded, sweating profusely and reeking of the champagne that had been poured liberally over me there wasn't all that much I could do to stop Alex and his mean buddies from getting the drop on me.

"OHHHHHHH yeah, shooting my fucking load now you bastards!!" I garbled throatily as Dennis stroked me and stroked me.

I spewed a third mess of frothy jock boy cum. Alex, Ronald, Dennis and Rodd, the four guys in Alex's dorm room cheered me on jovially and mockingly. My cum landed all over my chest, mixing with the messes from earlier and the ice cream and beer. As soon as I was done and before I could catch my breath Alex yanked my head back and shoved the damned funnel in my mouth for what seemed like the umpteenth time that afternoon.

"Fr-*frucker,*" I blurted around the edges of the funnel.

"More beer for the heroic captain!!" Alex said to Ronald.

This time I was force-fed two bottles of brew. I tried my best to chug it down, but a lot of it wound up dripping all over me. I squirmed miserably in that chair, as chills coursed through me and my head spun and spun. As I guzzled the beer I thought back to how I had come to wind up in this God-awful position. And Ronald was right with what he'd said earlier. Didn't any of the guys on my team realize that I was missing? But fuck me hard buds, even if those guys did realize it I doubted that they would think to look for me in Alex's dorm room…

As I said earlier my name is Johnny Richardson. I'm twenty-one years old, student and captain of the football team at the college that I attend. I have light brown wavy hair, dark brown chestnut shaped eyes and my body is rock hard and totally muscular from the constant workouts I punish myself through daily. On the day that I am telling you about my team was scheduled to play a game of football on the turf of one of our neighboring colleges. On the bus ride to the campus we all joked and swore how we were going to make short work of the opposing team. We were on our way to being the college champions after all. And fuck it all, we sure as shit beat the tar out of them. It gave us all a great thrill and feeling of ecstasy to have beaten them on their home turf let me tell you. After I had made the winning play (I think that was the first thing the losing team held against me) three of my strongest players hoisted me to their shoulders and carried me across the field to the visiting team's locker room. I was waving my hands and arms in the air triumphantly as people from our college cheered in the stands. The losing team's spectators booed and ranted. As I was being carried across the field I saw Alex and Ronald standing there looking totally dejected, their football helmets in their hands. The way they were looking up at me atop my teammate's shoulders should have warned me that they had something wicked and evil in mind for me. Unfortunately I didn't think anything of the looks on their faces at that time. In the locker room my teammates put me down and we sprayed each other liberally with bottles upon bottles of champagne. We poured it over each other in triumph. I got most of it, as I was the captain. When I was stripped to my boxer shorts and sweat socks one of my best players hoisted me to his shoulders and carried me around the locker room. Strong fucker that guy is for sure. I was doused with more and more champagne, slapped on the butt and congratulated over and over on being one of the best college football captain's around. While I was busy being celebrated and lifted to other guy's shoulders and carried around like a king the other members of the team were taking showers, getting dressed and anticipating the welcome they would receive when we all arrived back at our campus. While I was riding high on one of the guy's shoulders I had no fucking idea that I would not be accompanying my teammates back to our campus. By the time the rest of the team was dressed and ready to go I was still standing there in my boxer shorts and sweat socks, looking real sweet and sexy, HA! I hadn't even packed my football gear into my big, hugely over-sized duffel bag. *Shit, I* was going to be packed into my damned duffel bag.

"Hey Johnny! We'll see you on the bus," one of my players shouted at me from the end of the row of lockers I was standing in front of.

"Okay man!" I shouted back, waving at him and another guy as they exited the locker room.

When I was alone I sat down on the long bench in front of my locker to relax for a few moments before showering. I figured the team would just have to wait for me. I was the captain after all and it's always cool to return to your home campus a tad late, fashionably late if you would. I looked at my football uniform strewn over the floor in front of my locker and I was swept up by a feeling of total pride. My body was tired and my muscles all felt strained from the long and grueling game but I was totally pumped up with pride. Sweat and champagne dripped all over my smooth muscular and well-toned torso. I was ripe with the scents of all of it let me tell you. When I stood up to shuck off my boxers I heard the sound of the locker room door being opened and then closed again.

"Hey, one of you guys forget something?" I called out with my hands on my sides of my boxers. "Don't be leaving anything here in the visiting team's locker room you guys. Knowing these guys you won't see your shit again." I stood there listening for a response and when none came I felt a slight pang of nervousness.

"Hey! Anybody there?" I called out.

Suddenly, from around the corner of the lockers Alex and Ronald appeared. They were each holding full bottles of champagne.

"Congratulations on the win Johnny boy, oh Johnny boy," Alex said tauntingly, popped the cork on his bottle and aimed it at me, followed quickly by Ronald.

"UHHHHFFF," I grunted as I was pelted with freezing cold champagne, backing away from them on my socked feet. "WH-what is this? The losing team's player's showering the winning team's captain with champagne? I never heard of this shit before! WH-what the fuck is going on Alex?"

As I backed up Alex and Ronald continued showering me with the champagne, adding to the mess of it that was already all over me. Suddenly, from behind, Dennis and Rodd grabbed my upper arms, two more players from the opposing team.

"H-huh???" I grunted in surprise as they meanly yanked my big tired and muscular arms behind me.

Alex and Ronald moved closer to me, holding what was left of the contents in the champagne bottles.

"WH-what is this?" I asked, feeling a little more than nervous at that point.

I was sure they were going to be totally sore losers and beat the fucking fuck out of me right then and there. But instead Ronald yanked my head back and forced the tip of his bottle of champagne into my mouth. As I was held tightly and fast I was forced to guzzle cheap champagne.

"GGRRRRRMMMFFF!!!" I snorted.

"What you said was true," Alex said mockingly and brazenly squeezed one of my big pink fleshy nipples.

"And what the fuck might that have been?" I asked him angrily as Dennis and Rodd held my muscular arms tighter behind me.

"About the guys from your team leaving shit in the visiting team's locker room star boy, oh Johnny boy," Alex said and squeezed my nipple again, harder this time and twisting it as well. "They made a huge mistake leaving you in here all alone Johnny boy, oh Johnny boy. They aren't going to be seeing you for quite a while."

A look of terror came over my face when I realized just what the four guys had in mind for me.

"Just what we'll need for carting his ass to my dorm room," Alex said and picked up my huge over-sized duffel bag.

"Oh shit, NO," I gasped and tried in vain to pull out of Dennis and Rodd's grasps. "WH-what the fuck is this all about guys?"

"Just want to give the captain of the winning team a time he'll never forget," Alex said, holding my duffel bag wide open. "Tie him up and gag him real well guys."

"T-tie me up???" I gasped louder. "Alex, you have got to be fucking joking!"

Ronald reached into his jeans pockets and brought out a few long lengths of rope and a ratty pair of sweaty looking used white sweat socks. No doubt they were his socks from the game that we had just played.

"OOOHHHRRR SHIT, shit, you bastards," I seethed, realizing that I had been duly snagged by the sore losers of the opposing team. "What kind of shit is this? Kidnap the captain of the winning team?"

"Actually we were going to snag whoever of your team was left last in here," Alex said as Ronald got busy roping my hands tightly behind me. "As the captain of the team you should be glad it's you we're snagging rather than one of your cute players out there."

"Goddamn you Alex!!" I seethed through clenched teeth. "My players will get you for this!"

"HA, but will they get you Johnny boy, oh Johnny boy?" Alex tauntingly replied and again twisted one of my nipples.

"Get off my nips you prick!" I spat at him.

When my hands were tied Dennis and Rodd let go of my arms and Ronald squatted to tie my socked feet together.

"Alex, you can't mean this man!!" I ranted helplessly, looking down and watching Ronald tie my feet. "This is sick!! Just what the fuck are you planning on doing with me?"

"Stuff that your mind can't even imagine Johnny boy, oh Johnny boy," Alex said. "Gag him now. I don't want to hear shit from him till we're all safely in my dorm room."

Ronald handed the mangy sweat socks to Dennis. He rolled one of them into a ball and forced it deeply into my mouth, effectively gagging me. The sock tasted of sweat and putridly funky.

"RRRMMMFFFFF!!!" I grunted angrily, sneering meanly at Alex, the goddamned ringleader.

Dennis tied the other sock over the one crammed in my mouth, jamming it firmly in place. My cock pounded hard and big in fear in my boxers as I stood there being tied and gagged. When Ronald was done he stood up straight and looked at Alex.

"All done," Ronald said and patted me on the chest. "All tied and packaged and ready to go."

The four guys laughed meanly as Alex and Ronald held the duffel bag widely open. Terror filled my eyes even more-so now as I looked at Alex and Dennis and Rodd hoisted me up off the floor by my upper arms. This time I would not be riding in triumph upon anyone's shoulders.

They slid me into the huge duffel bag feet first and forced me down to a squatting position inside it. They pulled the top of it shut and tied the ends of it together.

"Okay, let's get out of here and get to my dorm room," Alex said.

I felt pairs of hands hoist the duffel bag and then I was slung across someone's shoulders like a damned sack of laundry. I was carried through the locker room and out to where my teammates were on the buses, waiting for the ride back to our campus.

"WHOOOOOO!!! Hey you guys, good game!!" I heard one of my players calling mockingly to Alex and his buddies, not knowing that their team captain was being abducted…and right under their very noses at that.

"Yeah, better luck next time!!" I heard another of my players call out.

"Good game!!" Alex called out in reply to them and slapped my butt hard.

"RRRMMMFFFF!!!" I gasped in total anguish as I was kidnapped right before the eyes of my team.

For all they knew Alex was carting a load of dirty football uniforms to the laundry room. When they turned a corner I sensed that all four of my captors breathed a collective sigh of relief. Disbelief set in hard and heavy. I had just been kidnapped right before the eyes of my teammates.

"We made it, I cannot fucking believe our luck," Alex said happily. "We didn't just snag one of their players; we fucking got their damned handsome captain."

Amid the sounds of mean laughter I was carted along toward Alex's dorm room and outright miserable torture…

When we arrived in Alex's dorm room, which was on the first floor of the building the duffel bag was instantly untied and Alex shook me out of it as if I were a sack of dirty laundry.

"RRRMMMFFFF!!!" I sputtered angrily up at him, as I lay there splayed on the floor.

The awful taste of the moist sweat socks crammed in my mouth had me livid at that point, not that there was much I could do about it though.

"Man, this is just too much to be believed," Alex said in awe, looking at me hungrily. "The captain of the opposing team, talk about luck."

Ronald placed a wooden straight backed chair in the center of the room as Dennis and Rodd pulled me meanly to my tied feet.

"Your throne Captain," Ronald quipped, pointing at the chair I was to be tied to.

"Not just yet Ronald," Alex said. "I want to plug his butt hole first. Fucking muscled Johnny boy, oh Johnny boy is going to hell in a hand basket."

"RRRRRMMMFFFF!!!" I gasped loudly and in shock when I saw the big fat pink butt-plug that Alex produced from a desk drawer.

I had to wonder where that fucking device had been...

"Heh, heh, you're not going to believe how this thing is going to feel when I push it into that sweet asshole of yours Captain," Alex said and then looked at Dennis and Rodd who were still standing at my sides.

They were holding my upper arms real tight, keeping me well balanced on my tied feet.

"Untie his big feet, spread those legs of his and moisten his hole boys," Alex said commandingly. Dennis and Rodd instantly did as they were told. My eyes opened in total shock at that point as I stood there now with my legs spread wide like a cheap whore's and the two guys were squatting behind me. GAWD, they were taking turns drooling in my rancid stink hole and flicking their tongues around in there. My boxers had been pulled down in the back, exposing my creamy white round butt cheeks as the guys took turns eating my ass chowder.

"RRRMMMFFFF, *fraggots!!*" I seethed into my sock gag.

I balled my tied hands into fists as Dennis and Rodd really went to town eating my damned hole. Alex stood a few feet away from me holding that damned butt-plug in his hand, mocking me with it. Dennis and Rodd held my ass cheeks apart and took greedy turns meanly sucking and lapping at my gaping hole of raunchy. After a while it was more than moist but the guys went on and on eating it anyway, treating my hole almost as if it were a pussy.

"Bet that's feeling real good eh muscle boy?" Alex asked me as I stood there with my back arched, looking up at the ceiling in disbelief.

The two guys eating my hole playfully snapped the elastic in my sweat soaked white sweat socks and ran their mangy hands up and down my legs. Then, Alex stepped behind me as well and as Dennis and Rodd held my cheeks spread the guy slowly inserted the butt-plug into my gaping and wet hole.

"MMMMFFFFF!!!" I wailed and Ronald stepped in front of me.

He placed a hand over the hard bulge that I was sporting in my champagne soaked boxer shorts.

"Say Alex, he really is enjoying all this shit," Ronald said and in a fast move he had my big cock and equally big juicy balls hanging out of the fly opening of my boxers. "Just look at this goddamned boner he's got."

Alex slid the butt-plug home into my hole, the round base of it sticking out like a handle of sorts. He gave one of my ass cheeks a tight painful squeeze followed by a stinging slap. Dennis pulled my boxers back up in the back and Alex was right. I could not believe the feeling of that thing wedged inside me. My cock was rock hard in Ronald's hand as Alex stepped in front of me.

"Fuck man, he's oozing pre cum," Alex said amazement. "Jack him the fuck off Ronald, and then we'll get him roped to the chair and really get this party going."

I stood there squirming in my socks as Ronald began slowly stroking my hard cock. Dennis and Rodd stood behind me and took turns squeezing my butt cheeks and slapping them hard a few times as well. Smiling, Alex took the sock gag out of my mouth. I licked my dried lips a few times before saying anything.

"You fucking bastards, you kidnappers!!" I seethed miserably, watching Ronald stroke me and stroke me. "Fucking guys' man, not only did you turn practical jokers, you also turned faggots!! OHHHHHHHH GAWDS, I'm fucking getting close already you guys!!"

Ronald stroked my big beefy cock faster and faster. I stood there sweating and stinking like crazy and then shot a load big enough to choke a fucking horse.

"OHHHHHH YEAH, fucking A you faggots!" I seethed miserably as I shot my load all over my big muscular chest, Ronald holding my cock straight up. "OHHHHHH, g-got me creaming like a bitch in heat."

As I shot rope upon rope of thick creamy college-boy sperm the butt-plug wedged in my hole drove me crazy to put it bluntly. Goose bumps broke out all over me and I came to discover just how sensitive a guy's hole becomes after having just shot a load. If that said guy has something big wedged in his hole it drives his poor hole even crazier. I grunted and roared in forced passion as Ronald squeezed every possible drop of jazz out of my cock slit. When I was done Ronald let go of my manhood and as I gasped for breath Alex took me by my upper arms.

"It has nothing to do with being faggots," he said into my ear, his lips practically grazing my earlobe. "It has to do with teaching the captain of the winning team a humiliating lesson."

"Fucking sore losers," I seethed as Alex moved me toward the chair.

Once I was seated the four guys got busy roping me tightly to the chair. My spent cock churned and the butt-plug in my hole seemed to move in further once I was sat down.

"Alex, what's the point of all this?" I called out to him as he opened a small refrigerator on the other side of the room.

"Well, we just wanted to have a party with one of the members of the winning team," Alex said and took three large gallon-sized ice cream buckets out of the refrigerator followed by a few six packs of beer. "And I for one am so fucking glad that we nailed the captain of the winning team that I could just shoot my wad right now."

"Like I said before man, fucking sore losers you all are!!" I ranted through clenched teeth.

I watched as Alex set the three gallons of ice cream and the six packs of beer on a table in front of the chair I was now securely tied to. From another drawer he produced three ice cream scoops and that blasted funnel that he and his cronies would use to force me to chug beer.

"Now, all three flavors of this ice cream have been liberally, *very liberally* I might add, laced with rum," Alex said to me, leaning down over me and tweaking my nipples as he spoke. "How much of it do you think we're going to have to scoop into you before you're stinking drunk?"

"A-Alex, you, you wouldn't," I whimpered as he twisted and tweaked the fucks out of my nipples. "GAWD, easy with my tits you bastard!"

My cock began to get hard again as it hung there outside my boxer shorts along with my succulent balls.

"And after we've got you all drunk and in a stinking lather and a half we'll bring you back to your campus," Alex went on, still holding tightly to my nipples, mashing them and pulling on them at that point. "AND, HA, you'll be wearing one of OUR football uniforms. Lets see how your team feels when they find you wearing one of our damned uniforms."

"Alex, you fucking sinister bastard," I seethed at him through clenched teeth.

He let go of my nipples and looked at me fiendishly.

"Let the fun begin," Alex called out and all four of the guys took ice cream scoops in hand.

They pried open the three buckets of ice cream and they each scooped out a good helping of it. I sat there bound up shivering in fear and anger. Alex went first; forcing a scoop of rum laced vanilla ice cream into my mouth, past my trembling lips. I gulped it down as quickly as possible as chills sped through me. Ronald then force-fed me rum-laced chocolate ice cream and I swallowed that quickly as well. When all four of the guys had each fed me a scoop of the rum laced ice cream my head was already spinning. The taste of rum in the dairy treat was overwhelming to say the least. What I could not swallow of the ice cream was dripping from my chin and down onto my big muscular chest. Alex held my head back by a handful of my hair as Ronald held the funnel wedged in my mouth and Rodd did the honors of pouring the first of the cold beers into me.

"GGGRRRRMMMFFFF!!!" I sputtered miserably as I chugged down the freezing cold beer.

I burped mightily in between chugging the beer and what I could not swallow of that also dripped down my chin and onto my chest. Dennis was squatting at my side and the fucking pervert had my big fat cock in his hand. I gasped and heaved as the fucker delighted in stroking me up to yet another good and throbbing boner. With my head being held back

I could not see, but felt it as the fucking guy slathered his tongue over my big stinking and sweating testicles. He stroked me harder and harder and harder, DAMN! I squirmed on that damned butt-plug and tried to swallow beer at the same time. When the first bottle of beer was gone Alex let go of my hair and I faced forward. Looking down at Dennis I grimaced in anger and frustration.

"GAWD, look at you, fucking faggot can't seem to leave my damned cock alone," I seethed. "OHHHHHH FUCK, getting there again you bastards!!"

With that I let fly with a second good-sized load of football player spunk.

"OHHHHHHH GAWD, oh fucking A you bastards!!" I roared with my mouth wide open.

While my mouth was hanging open Alex took that opportunity to force-feed me another hefty scoop of the rum laced ice cream. My head spun as I chugged it down and finished shooting my load of slop at the same fucking time.

"Down the hatch Johnny boy, oh Johnny boy," Alex teased me as I swallowed the ice cream.

"RRRRRMMMFFFF!!!" I sputtered loudly as my stomach churned.

When I was done shooting my load all over my sticky messy chest Dennis let go of my cock and all four of the guys again force-fed me a scoop of ice cream each. The taste of the rum mixed with the ice cream was acrid now and I was starting to feel pretty cold. The butt-plug tormented my poor hole no end after having shot that second load. My head was spinning after still more ice cream was fed to me and I was forced to guzzle two more bottles of beer through the funnel. Or was it three more? Shit, I lost count at some point.

So there you have it, that's how I came to wind up in this totally fucked up joke of a mess. After shooting my third load and being force-fed more ice cream/rum and beer the four guys decided to take a short breather. I sat there shivering and sweating miserably in the bondage. Remnants of ice cream dripped off my chin and down onto my chest. I saw that the buckets of ice cream were all only a quarter or so of the way done so far. I silently prayed that they didn't plan to force-feed me all three gallons of the ice cream. I would be farting my guts out for days if they did that. There was still plenty of beer left as well. Shit, I was already pretty sopped at that point and I wondered just how much more Alex and his buddies planned on doing to me. All four of them were standing around me at that point, tweaking my nipples, rubbing my sticky chest and stealing pulls and tugs on my cock and balls.

"Great party huh guys?" Alex asked his cronies.

"Sure as shit man," Ronald said gleefully. "Looks like this guy is pretty drunk already."

"I don't want him pretty drunk, I want him stinking drunk," Alex said meanly. "When we give him back to his teammates they are not going to believe the shape they find him to be in."

My stomach churned and I managed to hold back a fart as I squirmed on the damned butt-plug.

"SH-sh, shit," I whimpered. "TH-this is worse than hell week."

All four of the guys laughed and guffawed meanly, slapped me on the back and playfully snapped the elastic in my boxers against my skin.

"Okay guys, time to resume the party," Alex said and scooped out a good helping of ice cream for me.

"OHHHH GAWD," I mumbled loudly and miserably and then gasped as Dennis squatted in front of me and wrapped his lips meanly around one of my poor aching balls.

I was force-fed what seemed like endless scoops upon scoops of the rum laced ice cream, forced to chug beer upon beer through a funnel all the while having my damned testicles slurped and sucked on. My cock throbbed hard and wildly and when I did fart all the guys whooped and screamed about how bad it stunk.

"Looks like our star boy here better use the bathroom before we take him to his campus," Alex said as he started untying me.

When I was untied Dennis and Rodd held me balanced as Alex slowly slid the butt-plug out of my hole. It came out with a soft squishing sound followed by yet another fart. I was feeling totally humiliated and beyond mortified at that point. But there was no time to think about that. In my drunken stupor I pulled out of Dennis and Rodd's grasps and shambled madly to the bathroom amid the raucous laughter, hoots and cackling of all four of the guys who had kidnapped me…

In the bathroom I pissed like crazy into the bowl and then the need to sit down was overwhelming…

When I was done in the bathroom I emerged slowly, my head still spinning and feeling pretty drunk and sloshed. The cum, beer, sweat and ice cream had caked up all over my chest. Alex and his buddies grabbed me as I exited the bathroom and I was too damned drunk to realize that they were dressing me in one of their football team uniforms. I was forced into a football jersey with their team name on the front of it. I was made to step into the knickers style pants of the football uniform. Shoulder pads were put on me as well as a pair of football cleats. As a finishing touch they tied a black silk blindfold over my eyes before putting the football helmet with the team logo on it on my head. I didn't struggle all that much as I was pretty damn drunk and in no position whatsoever to struggle as it was. But they roped my arms tightly together at the biceps anyway.

"Okay guys, lets get the star boy here to his campus," Alex said. "I'm sure there's a party going and in full swing over there by now."

That said Alex hoisted me across his big shoulders. I farted loudly and all the guys laughed and hooted again…

In the gym of the college that I attend *there was* a party going on and in full swing. The entire team was there along with our coaches and many of the college professors and instructors. Outside the gym Alex slid me off his shoulders and to my wobbly feet as Ronald opened the gym door part of the way. Alex held my bound arms tightly as Ronald checked out the scene in the gym.

"Okay, let's just shove him the fuck in there and be on our way," Alex said.

He let go of my arms, reached through the plastic grid on the opposing team helmet that I was wearing and took the blindfold off me.

"Al-Alex, don't, don't do this," I begged. "Pl-please man."

Snickering meanly, Alex pushed me through the partly opened door of the gym. The door closed behind me and I shambled stupidly into the gym.

"Hey, check this shit out!!" one of my players called out gleefully, grabbing me by my bound arms. "Looks like someone got the drop on one of the guys from the opposing team!"

"Steve, no, it, it's me," I managed to say softly.

"Let's see who we have here," Steve said and yanked the helmet off my head.

When the helmet was off me I was faced with looks of disbelief and shock.

"SHIT!! Captain Richardson, wh-what happened?" Steve asked me. "Why, why the fuck are you wearing that uniform?"

"I, they, fucking bastards!!" was all I could manage to say in my drunken state.

I felt the need to fart coming on and I wanted to be away from the entire crowd quickly, before that eruption happened.

"SH-Shteve, you and Mike, get me down to the locker room, fast," I said drunkenly. "I-I'll try to explain all this later, *when I'm wearing a proper uniform!!*"

Steve and Mike, two of my best players hustled me down to the locker room. Halfway there I farted miserably and uncontrollably.

"F-fucking bastards from the opposing team kidnapped me," I grunted and burped loudly as we walked into the locker room. "Fuckers got me sloshed and drunk you guys, perverts even jacked me off a few times, can you beat that? Fuck man, and they, they fucking dressed me up in one of their stinking uniforms! What a way to be seen! I'd rather they had dressed me up like a girl, JEEZ!"

I hadn't mentioned the fact that Alex and his cronies had butt-plugged my hole. I felt that what I had told my buddies and the way they had seen me clad in the opposing team's uniform was more than enough information for them.

"Holy shit!!" Steve said. "What a shitty ass thing to do to the captain of the football team."

"G-get me untied you guys," I said desperately. "I-I have to piss like a goddamned racehorse!!"

"Sure thing Captain," Mike said and my two best players untied me.

"I'll take a shower and then I'll be up to join the party," I said as I moved quickly toward the bathroom. "Tell the coaches I'll explain everything then."

"Sure thing Captain," Mike said and he and Steve went back up to the gym.

After taking a long, mean and frothy piss I walked slowly over to my locker. I still couldn't believe what the fuck had happened to me, SHIT, kidnapped and worked over by guys from the losing team. My head was spinning, I was fucking sloshed, but I was sure I would be able to get myself under some sort of control after a shower. I quickly stripped out of the opposing team uniform down to my boxers and sweat socks. Actually, to tell it plainly I couldn't get the fucking thing off myself fast enough. I took a towel from my locker and walked toward the shower room. As I passed the spot where Mike and Steve had untied me and threw the rope on the floor my heart leapt in my chest. OH GAWD, the rope was gone. Suddenly, Alex and Ronald appeared from around the corner of a row of lockers along with Dennis and Rodd.

"Hello Captain," Alex snickered.

I gulped hard. JEEZ, letting me go so quick was just a ploy, just a rouse to get me all pumped up so they could nab my sorry ass again. In what seemed like moments they had me bound hand and foot all over again, and gagged. Alex and his buddies, laughing meanly carted my sexy ass right out of the team locker room and back to Alex's dorm room for more of what they had dished out on me earlier. They had left the opposing team uniform that I had been wearing hanging on my locker door for all my teammates to see, if they happened to go down to the locker room. It wasn't until the next day that I saw my teammates again...

THE PLAINCLOTHES POLICEMAN

My name is Michael Putman, Officer Michael Putman to be more exact. I'm a plainclothes police officer with the New York City police force. I'm about five feet ten inches tall; I have brown wavy hair, a thick mustache and a messy looking beard. I'm in fairly good shape except for a slight pot belly. My chest however is pretty robust and hairy, a real guy's chest, fuck yeah! Girlfriends of mine over the years have told me that the combination of a big hairy chest and a slight belly is somewhat sexy. I'm thirty eight years old. I've worked on such cases as catching purse snatchers in parks, pickpockets in the subway, and even protecting the homeless. But nothing and I mean nothing had prepared me for the case I took a few months ago. It was a Monday morning and when I entered the precinct I was told by the cop at the front desk that Sergeant Green wanted to see me immediately. Dressed in jeans, high top sneakers, and a sweatshirt I walked quickly to my sergeant's office. I knocked twice and he bellowed for me to come in.

"Good morning Putman," he said to me, pointing to a chair in front of his desk.

"Good morning Sir," I said and saluted him before sitting down. He returned the salute.

Sergeant Green was a big man with graying hair and blue eyes. I guessed his age to be somewhere in his mid forties.

"I was told you wanted to see me immediately Sir," I said to Green.

"Yes I did Putman," he replied. "I'm going to get right to the point.

Have you ever had any homosexual experiences Putman?"

I shifted nervously in the chair, pursed my lips and then said, "Sir?"

"Ever had your cock sucked by a guy?" he asked me bluntly and meanly. "Ever had a guy lick your nipples, fuck your asshole? Ever fucked a guy in his asshole?"

"This is a joke right Sir?" I asked him. "My buddies out there put you up to this right? A joke?"

"No joke Putman, no joke," Green replied. "We've had numerous reports of a rapist on the loose in the Greenwich Village area. He rapes men Putman, gay men. I would like to send you into the gay community to try to flush this guy out."

"Me? Why me Sir?" I asked after a gulp.

"You're his type Putman," Green said to me. "All the men he's gone after are your height, have a beard and mustache, and dress pretty casually."

"Why can't someone just identify him?" I asked, hoping to avoid this case.

"Because it sounds like that when he approaches his victims he's wearing a fake mustache or a fake beard and glasses," Green explained. "Then, after he has his victim drugged and in his car the fucker blindfolds them and keeps them blindfolded till he's done doing what it is he does to the poor sap."

"And uh, just what exactly does the fucker do to the poor sap?" I asked, playing nervously with my mustache.

"We've had mixed reports," Green said. "One guy said that he fucked him in the ass while he was tied up and blindfolded, another guy says that he sucked his cock numerous times, forcing him to ejaculate till it became really painful, another guy says that the rapist spent the evening sucking his toes…"

"Shit…" I said softly. "And you want me to go after this pervert…"

"Yeah, just don't wind up as one of his victims," Green replied.

"Do I get some time to think about it?" I asked.

"Sure, let me know by this afternoon if you want to take the case," Green said. "If you don't I'm going to be hard up to find another plainclothes man who fits your description."

"Okay, thanks," I said and stood up.

I walked out of Green's office and went to a nearby coffee shop to think it over. As I sat there sipping coffee and slowly eating a donut I thought about all the reported cases of women being raped that we always heard about. But men...men being raped...I could not believe it. Imagine being forced to shoot your load numerous times. Man, it would take a magician to do that to me. At thirty eight years old I found that after shooting my load I was done for the night, hardy har, har. Being fucked in the ass...man that was just unthinkable. I could not even imagine a big cock in my small asshole. And having your toes sucked all night...now that was something I wouldn't mind having a woman do to me. A guy raping men...I could not believe it. I decided to take the case...

That afternoon I returned to Sergeant Green's office and told him I would take the job. I was instructed that I was not to carry a gun or a badge. I would report only to Green on my progress. I asked him how this rapist met the men he victimized.

"Three of the victims say they met him in a bar called Uncle Charlie's, that's on Greenwich Avenue in the village," Green replied. "One of the other victims says that he met the rapist in a gay dance club called The Monster, that's on Grove Street and Seventh Avenue in the village."

I toyed with my mustache, realized that this guy was using the New York club and bar scene to lure his victims and told Green that I would start with The Monster. I liked dance music. Green told me to be careful and not to react harshly if any of the gay men in the club came on to me.

"I'll be fine Sir," I said as I left his office and jokingly blew him a kiss.

Green laughed and wished me luck.

That night I arrived at the Monster clad in a pair of faded blue jeans with a rip on the left thigh of the jeans, a matching button down shirt with the top four buttons unbuttoned and the shirt tails pulled out of my jeans, and a pair of beige Dockers with no socks. I paid the five dollar admission charge at the door and walked into the club. I found a spot at the bar and ordered a Bud light. The bartender handed me the beer and I handed him a five dollar bill, telling him to keep the change. I looked around as I sipped my beer. The place was filled with a wide variety of men. Men in business suits, men dressed in jeans like me, construction workers, and older men as well. In the back of the bar a man played a piano while some of the men gathered around the piano sang an old Judy Garland song. I smiled. I liked Judy Garland. She was cool, or had been cool. On the floor I could feel the thumping of the music from the dance floor below. That was where I would go next I decided. As I went to stand up a hand rested on one of my shoulders. I turned to see a man in his mid forties standing next to me. He was dressed in a navy blue business suit.

"Hello there," he said happily. "I don't believe I've ever had the pleasure of seeing you here before."

I smiled at him and resumed my seat.

"I'm Lester," he said.

"I'm Michael," I replied and shook hands with him. "Would you uh, would you like to sit down?"

"No, I'm fine," Lester said. "But may I buy you a drink?"

"I don't see why not," I said. "I'm drinking Bud light."

Lester signaled the bartender and ordered a second beer for me. I thanked him. Could he be the rapist? Could this mild mannered guy be the one who had been luring men into his clutches and brutally raping them? Would I have gotten that lucky my first night out? As I sipped my beer Lester asked me what I did for a living. He was making small talk, wanting to find out the quickest way to get into my pants. I told him that I worked as a maintenance man in an office building. Lester in turn told me that he was a vice president with Chase Manhattan Bank and went on to brag about all his responsibilities. We talked for about an hour, mostly about him. A few times his hand found its way to my leg but didn't linger long. After a while Lester said that it had been nice meeting me and walked over to the piano to join in the singing. I smiled and took a hearty gulp of my third beer.

"Nope, he's definitely not the rapist..." I mused to myself.

I decided at that point to go to the dance floor. From behind me I heard a voice say, "He's a stupid old fool."

I turned and saw a man of about twenty five years old standing next to me. He had brown hair and brown eyes. He was a little taller than me and had a thin mustache.

"I'm sorry…" I said to him. "Were you talking to me?"

"Yeah, I'm Roy," he said, taking my hand and shaking it. "Lester is an old fool. Just likes to hear himself talk.

"You know him?" I asked Roy who was still holding my hand in his.

"Yeah, he hit on me a few times in the past," Roy said, finally letting go of my hand. "He talks a lot of talk but then hardly ever follows through on it. What's your name by the way?"

"I'm Michael," I said.

"Nice to meet you Michael," Roy said. "Can I get you another beer?"

"Sure," I replied.

Man, my first time in a gay bar and two guys had bought me drinks. While Roy ordered a beer for me I excused myself to the men's room. When I came back my beer was waiting for me and so was Roy. He had a beer in front of him also. We clinked our bottles together and drank to new friendships.

"So, tell me more about Lester," I said to Roy, thinking that maybe Lester was the rapist after all.

"What's to tell?" Roy asked, sounding annoyed. "He's just a guy who's too full of himself."

I took a mouthful of my beer and suddenly felt dizzy.

"You however is a totally different story Michael," Roy said, placing a hand on my exposed chest.

His fingers toyed deliberately with my chest hairs and he leaned toward me.

"You are beautiful Michael," he whispered to me, his fingers roaming on my chest and finding a nipple and squeezing it. "Did anyone ever tell you that?"

"N-no," I replied, feeling more dizzy. "H-hey, I feel dizzy…"

"It's warm in here," Roy said. "Maybe you need some air. Come on, I'll help you outside…"

From the corner of my eye I saw Lester at that piano. He was smiling fiendishly as Roy helped me out of the bar, holding me tightly by my arms. Outside, the air didn't help. I still felt very dizzy. When I tried to tell Roy that I felt dizzier he pulled me close to himself and kissed me full on the lips. God, I had never kissed a man before but somehow I was not repulsed by it at all. Roy's tongue gently found its way between my lips and into my mouth. He sucked at my tongue like a madman. No one passing by seemed to notice us. It was Greenwich Village after all. Who would care? When Roy stopped kissing me he walked me over to a car and sat me in the passenger seat. As he climbed into the driver's seat he took a small spray can out of his jeans pocket.

"I drugged your beer Michael," he said to me. "And now you're mine."

Before I could say anything he sprayed the contents of the spray can he was holding in my face. I fell into unconsciousness...

When I came to a while later I was still in Roy's car...only now my hands were roped tightly behind me and I was blindfolded. As I came around I realized that what Sergeant Green had warned me about had happened, I had been captured by the rapist.

"Ohhhhhhhh..." I moaned miserably as I came to.

"Feeling okay?" Roy asked as he drove.

"Wh-where are you taking me?" I asked weakly. "What is going on???"

"I'm taking you to my apartment for some fun Michael my boy," Roy snickered. "We're almost there..."

Again, he sprayed knockout gas, or whatever the fuck it was in my face and I fell back into the land of nod. A little while later I came to again while Roy was stopping the car. Roy knew that I was awake again by the sound of my moans.

"Th-that shit stinks," I stammered. "Quit spraying that at me..."

"It's only a mild knockout gas Michael," Roy said. "It won't kill you. Now, we're in the concourse level parking lot of my apartment building. I don't see anyone so I can probably get you upstairs with no problem..."

"Y-you're that rapist everyone is talking about..." I said as I heard Roy get out of the car.

He opened the passenger side door of the car and pulled me out by my arm, closing the car door.

"Okay, be real fucking quiet and I won't have to gag you Michael," Roy said threateningly. "We're going up the freight elevator.

Holding me by my arm Roy hustled me quickly into a freight elevator and then we were on our way up to his apartment.

"Lester set me up for you didn't he?" I asked Roy.

"He sure did," Roy replied. "You sure are one smart dude. Quite unlike the other brain-numb hunks I've encountered."

Roy pulled me close to him and as the elevator continued it's ascent he kissed me on the lips. Remarkably I found myself responding by kissing him back and pushing my tongue into his mouth. I felt my cock getting hard in my pants.

"MM..." Roy crooned. "We're going to have loads of fun. And judging from that hard-on in your jeans you're going to shoot a lot of loads."

The elevator stopped; on what floor I had no fucking idea. In what seemed like no time Roy had me in his apartment.

"Okay Michael, we're home," Roy said, guiding me through the apartment.

"Why am I blindfolded?" I asked him. "I've already seen your face."

"No you haven't Michael," Roy responded. "The mustache and hair you saw on me were false. No one I've kidnapped and raped has seen my face..."

With amazing strength Roy lifted me off the floor and stretched me out on a table on my back.

"Sleepy bye time again Michael," he said jokingly and sprayed the knockout gas in my face.

"UHHHHH..." I said and fell asleep.

The next time I came to I was still tied and blindfolded but I also was able to tell that Roy had stripped me down to my white underpants. I was still laying stretched out on the table and felt a tingling sensation at my feet. Fuck, Roy was sucking my toes one at a time and licking my big feet all over.

"OHHHHH..." I moaned as I came to again. "Roy, stop putting me to sleep. God, but that feels great..."

I had to admit to myself that it did feel great as Roy held one of my size eleven bare feet in his hands and worked it over with his tongue. I could feel my cock getting even harder in my briefs. I didn't wonder at the time what this made me. Was I gay or still straight? Had I ever been straight? My main concern at that moment was getting myself out of Roy's clutches and him into mine. I was the cop after all. But being tied and blindfolded I was pretty damned helpless to do much of anything.

And Roy had that damned knockout gas that he kept using on me...

"Your feet smell and taste nice and sweaty Michael," Roy said. "Wearing those Dockers with no socks sure does add to the aroma."

He slurped my pinkie toe into his mouth and sucked it ferociously. All I could do was moan in response. When Roy was done sucking each toe of my right foot and licking it all over he let go of it and grabbed my left foot.

"The last guy I had here had smaller feet than you Michael but I licked them anyway," Roy told me. "I simply love licking a man's feet. And the man before you had been wearing black nylon dress socks when I brought him here. I kept his socks as a souvenir. The guy before that shot five loads; count them, five loads, into his underpants with my help. I kept his under shorts as a souvenir."

"What are you going to keep as a souvenir in my case you pervert???" I asked him angrily.

"You Michael, I'm keeping you," Roy said. "I'm not letting you go, ever..."

I screamed "NO, NO, NO!!!" over and over as Roy began licking my left foot. He told me to scream all I wanted. The apartment was soundproof and that was why he hadn't gagged me. I stopped screaming and tried to remain calm.

"Wh-why do you want to keep me here for good?" I asked him.

"A few reasons," Roy replied. "You're incredibly handsome, I can see even under those briefs that you have been blessed with an enormous cock, and your feet are delicious."

"Roy, those are all really nice compliments man, but you'll go to jail, this is kidnapping, rape..." I said helplessly.

"Oh don't worry Officer Putman, no one will be looking for you so

I don't have much to worry about," Roy snickered.

"Officer?" I asked him in shock. "What do you mean Officer???"

"You're a cop Michael," Roy said to me. "Well, you were a cop, now your only mission in life will be to keep me happy."

How could he know I was a cop? I didn't have a badge on me; I was carrying a fake ID in my wallet... But then, a horrible realization hit me. It was when he had said that I had been wearing Dockers with no socks and how it had made the aroma of my feet even more sweaty and delicious. I should have realized it when he'd reminded me of my earlier footwear...

"Y-your name isn't Roy!!" I stammered and lifted my upper body slightly off the table. "I know who the fuck you are!!!"

Roy abandoned my foot and pushed me back down on the table with the palm of one of his hands.

"Uhhnnnnfff..." I said.

"Now that you know I really have to keep you forever Officer Putman," Roy said his lips close to mine.

"You bastard!!" I seethed. "WHY???"

Roy took my blindfold off me and I saw Sergeant Green smiling down at me. He stroked my beard and toyed with my mustache.

"I'm in love with you Putman," he said, still stroking my beard. "I have been ever since you first came on the force. I watched you go from a uniformed police officer to the plainclothes cop you are now. Your ambition and drive added to the drive I felt for you. But how could I make you see how I felt? I knew you were straight so I wouldn't stand a chance no matter what. Then, I decided I had to have you...no matter what, I had to have you. So, I abducted and raped various men who resembled you, hoping to cause a stir in the gay community. It worked. I told the commissioner that I would send one of my own men out there to nail this rapist. I told him I had just the man. He never asked for your name. He only wanted the rapist caught and gotten rid of. No one knows that I sent you out there Putman.

"Y-you raped those other men to get me to take the bait and take the case..." I whispered, not being able to speak normally at this point.

"Bingo," Green said, moving his hand down to one of my nipples and placing it between his thumb and first finger. "In a week or so when there are no more rapes I'll assure the commissioner that we've rid the streets of the rapist. I'll get all the credit and I'll have gotten you in the interim."

Green twisted my nipple a few times and then leaned down and gave it a few hearty sucks.

"UHHHHHH..." I grunted. "You did all this just so you could kidnap me???"

In response Green slurped my nipple hard between his teeth, rubbing the tip of his tongue against it.

"OHHHHH..." I moaned helplessly and in ecstasy.

"Green, you can't mean this!!" I said, finding my voice again. "People will realize I'm missing..."

Green stopped licking my foot again and holding my foot in his hands he looked at me and said, "Who?"

"Who is going to look for you Putman?" he asked me. "Your parents are dead, you have no brothers or sister, you live alone, you have no girlfriend, and you're really not close to anyone that I know of. You're basically a loner. I'll simply tell people that you resigned from the force and decided to move out of New York."

"You're insane," I said with my eyes opened wide in sheer terror now. "What about my apartment, all my stuff?"

"I'll inform your landlord that you've moved out and then I'll have all your stuff either sold or donated to worthy charities," Green replied, still holding my foot with his hand. "I'll have your mail forwarded to a PO Box and I'll pick it up on a weekly basis so you can pay off any outstanding bills and then eventually I'll have the mail stopped and you will officially disappear."

Green sniffed my foot a few times and then gobbled my big toe greedily into his mouth. He sucked my toe like a madman in heat. My cock throbbed long and hard, mostly from fear. I had to get away from him!!! But how??? I was totally powerless...

When Green finished with my feet he rolled a pair of black silk calf length socks onto them. He told me the socks belonged to the guy he'd told me about earlier. I felt a sense of kink wearing the socks of one of Green's other rape victims. The other victim who at the moment had his freedom...something that I was missing terribly already. Green gave each of my now black socked feet a kiss each and then moved to my crotch. He leaned down, kissed my underpants, and pulled them down a little, revealing my enormous, hard and throbbing member.

"Well, well, just as I always suspected, you are gargantuan!!" Green said in awe as he looked at my cock.

He closed a hand around it and held it tightly. It throbbed as if it was alive in his hand. Pre cum oozed out of my piss hole and slid down the shaft and I was breathless as I was handled.

"You're dying to shoot your load Putman," Green said jovially. "Do you want me to get you off?"

"I want you to let me go Sarge," I pleaded helplessly.

"Now Putman, you know that's not what is going to happen," Green said and slid my briefs down to my thighs.

He looked at my egg sized balls and let go of my cock. It pointed straight up and twitched as Putman gently rubbed the tips of his fingers against my aching cum filled balls.

"When was the last time you shot your load Putman?" he asked me.

I shrugged stupidly and said that it had been a few days, explaining that I liked to wait a few days between orgasms. It intensified it when I finally did cum. I could not believe that I was telling him all this.

"I'm going to make you wait a few more days Putman," Green said. "By that time you will be begging me to jack you off…and when I finally do you'll have a dildo wedged up in your ass. And then I'll make you wear the underpants of the guy who I forced to shoot five loads into his drawers. You'll add to his cum stains…

"You pervert!!" I shrieked, pulling my upper body off the table again. "You release me now!! I swear Sarge, I'll kill you!!! I WILL FUCKING KILL YOU!!!"

Green grabbed the can of knockout gas and sprayed it in my face. I fell back onto the table into unconsciousness…

When I came to a half hour later I saw that Green had put a different pair of underpants on me. I felt like his goddamned dress-up doll. He told me that they had belonged to the guy who he had forced to shoot his load five times into them. My cock was sticking out of the fly hole of the shorts along with my balls. Green explained that he didn't want anything rubbing against my erection and balls which could cause me to shoot my load sooner than he wanted me to. I looked at him helplessly and despondently. He had tied my upper body tightly to the table and was now busy licking, bighting, and nipping my nipples alternately. At this point my nipples were fully erect (like my cock I supposed) and pointy like two hard bullets jutted up on my chest. My feet were also tied now, adding to my helplessness. What would become of me if I didn't get out of this??? My cock throbbed, filled to capacity with cum, and begging for that cum to be released. My balls, equally as loaded up with jazz also throbbed maniacally. As I laid there wearing a stranger's underwear and another stranger's socks I felt the tears of fear flowing down my face.

On Tuesday morning Green allowed me to take a shower, brush my teeth, and shave. As I did all that he sat on the closed toilet, supervising me with the can of knockout gas in his hand. If I tried anything foolish all he would have to do was spray the gas in my face and render me unconscious. When I used the toilet Green stepped out of the bathroom but had told me to be wearing the socks and underwear he had given me the day before and the blindfold before exiting the bathroom. Man oh man, was I in a shit-load of trouble. When I came out of the bathroom I was wearing the socks and underwear and the blindfold. Green quickly roped my hands tightly behind me and tied my feet securely together. I stood there feeling helpless as my cock began to get hard again in the stranger's briefs. Green took my hardening cock out of the fly hole of the briefs along with my big juicy balls. Then, he lowered the briefs in the back, revealing my hairy butt. He hauled me up and over his shoulders and carried me through the apartment to his kitchen.

"UUUHHHFF…hey, take it easy Green," I said as he carried me. "You didn't have to tie my feet…I could have walked this trip."

Ignoring me Green sat me down at the kitchen table on a chair with a big vibrating dildo on it. Slowly, Green lowered my hole onto the dildo until I was rooted onto the damned thing, sitting on it if you would. The thing tormented my asshole and the vibrations it was giving off was sending massive chills through my body, causing goose-bumps to break out all over me.

"OHHHHRRRR GOD Green, what the hell is this???" I asked

breathlessly.

Green removed my blindfold for me and roped my thighs down to the chair, preventing me from getting up off the dildo. My cock was now hard as a fucking rock and crying pre-cum.

"That will tenderize your ass Michael," Green said to me, tugging on my mustache a few times.

He kissed me on the lips and then fed me breakfast. He gave me scrambled eggs, toast, and coffee. As he fed me I squirmed helplessly and miserably on the dildo.

"Green, please, jack me off once, please…" I begged, not believing myself what I had just said.

Green looked at me, smiled fiendishly, and laughed hysterically.

"Boy oh boy Putman, I thought it would take days or weeks to have you begging me for that," Green said. "It won't take long to train you at all. No, it's going to be a few days before you cum."

He patted me lovingly on the cheek and fed me more eggs. The bits and pieces of egg and toast that had landed in my mustache and beard Green picked out slowly. Later, he was dressed for work and I was stretched out on the table, tied down. Green had taken the dildo out of my ass and pulled the briefs back up in the back for me. My cock and balls remained sticking out of the fly hole.

"Green please, please man; think what you're doing…" I said to him as he stood there holding the can of knockout gas. "You can't keep me caged up like an animal!!"

Green simply smiled and sprayed the gas in my face.

As the days went by Green found more and more ways to torture me sexually. Everyday the vibrating dildo was up my ass for at least an hour, some days longer. Green loved watching me squirm and sweat on the damned thing. At other times Green would lick the sides of my pounding cock and balls. I thought that if I concentrated hard enough I could make myself cum without having my cock stroked or sucked. No such luck however. One day Green had roped me to the table and proceeded to tickle me everywhere with a variety of items he'd found in the apartment. Twice that first week I was given what Green called erotic spankings with a leather paddle. I called them painful spankings. My ass was always red and stinging. Green said that that was a good way to keep me reminded of who the commander in my life was now. On the eighth day Green said that he was finally going to allow me to shoot my load. I was sitting on the vibrating dildo and sweating profusely when he told me this.

"Please...please...jack me off now then..." I pleaded in a high pitched tone of voice. "I-I can't take it anymore!!"

Green slid the stranger's underpants over my throbbing cock and balls and began stroking me through the white cotton material. I rocked on the dildo as Green stroked me slowly. I came a few seconds later, shooting the biggest and most potent load of cop jazz out of my piss hole that I ever saw.

"OHHHHRRRRRR!!!" I screamed in wild passion. "OHHHHRRR GODS!!"

The cum filled the inside of the briefs and even seeped through the material. The cum that seeped through Green leaned down and licked into his mouth. Then, when I was done Green yanked my spent cock out of the briefs along with my balls and began jacking me off again.

"OH GOD NO!!" I screeched as Green used my own cum as a lubricant. "N-not again so fucking soon man!!"

But Green ignored me and stroked me harder. He was going to milk me dry. I sat there squirming on the dildo which had now become absolute torture and I was sweating like a crazed man. Green licked and bit my nipples a few times as he stroked and stroked my cock. I shot a second load into his hand.

"ORRRRRRRR you madman!!" I panted. "I'm cumming, again I'm cumming!!!"

Green forced two more cum shots out of me and then left me there panting for breath as he went to the bathroom to get ready for work...

A Year Later...

I still live with Sergeant Green and from all points it looks like I'll be living with him for the rest of my life. He has no intention of ever letting me go and I cannot possibly escape from him. He keeps me practically naked most of the time and uses the knockout gas on me constantly which keeps me pretty weak. Once every two weeks he jacks me off over and over till my balls are milked good and dry. I don't know which is worse, waiting to be jacked off or the actual milking. Everyday

I sit on the vibrating dildo for at least an hour now, no less. Every other day or so Green gives me a hard spanking on the ass till my ass cheeks shines red. He says that keeps me in line. As a reward I'm allowed to suck his cock, swallow his cum, and even drink his piss. Green fucks me on occasion but prefers to see me squirm on the vibrating dildo. Well, I have to stop now; Green just came into the room he keeps me in. He's carrying a blindfold which means I'm in for some new surprises...

A Boner Book

THE APARTMENT

What I want to tell you about happened last Friday at three AM. For whatever reason I couldn't sleep. I had

Woken up at two thirty AM and tossed and turned for a half hour before getting out of bed. I decided to sit up and read for a while… hoping that I would eventually fall back to sleep. As I walked past the window in my dark bedroom my attention was suddenly drawn to a light shining in my window. It was coming from the apartment building right across from the one I lived in. I stopped dead in my tracks when I saw what was happening in the apartment directly across from mine. I saw a tall guy standing in the middle of his living room. He was at least six feet tall…maybe a little more. He had brown wavy hair, a muscular chest and huge arms, and beautiful well-toned sexy legs. He was standing in the center of the living room dressed in just a pair of torn up white briefs. His muscular body was completely hairless. His long, fat hard cock was hanging out of the torn front of the briefs he was wearing. To make his situation even worse his hands were tied behind him and the rope was extended down behind him and tightly tied around a heavy looking weight that was on the floor at his feet. His feet were tied together and also roped to the weight. A ball separator was attached to his large hairy balls and to add to that there were ropes tied around his balls…also extended down and tied to the weight at the guy's feet. To top it all off he was blindfolded with a white cloth. I could not believe what I was seeing. Had someone kidnapped the guy or was he being held prisoner in his own apartment??? As the questions ran through my mind at sixty miles per hour I slid to my knees in front of the window. The guy looked so hot and sexual the way he was tied to that weight and totally immobilized. I could only imagine the pain his balls were in from the leather ball separator snapped on them and the ropes tied around them. He was taking deep breaths and from the look of the expression on his blindfolded face he was in pain. I was thinking about calling the police when suddenly I saw two men dressed in short black leather shorts, black leather vests, and black leather boots walk into the room where the bound and blindfolded guy was standing. They were both extremely muscular looking. One of them was carrying what looked like a metal bucket. He put the bucket down on the floor at the bound guy's feet and then the two leathermen began running their hands over the bound guy's chest, his arms, and neck. They squeezed his delectable and erect looking nipples and now from the look on the bound guy's blindfolded face it hurt pretty badly. He was only able to move his head and if he tried to move any other part of his body it would result in a nasty yank on his tortured balls. The two leathermen each grabbed one of the bound guy's arms and leaned in toward his chest. They both slurped one of his nipples into their mouth and chowed down heartily on them. The bound guy's cock grew harder and pre cum oozed out of his piss slit and down the sides of his shaft. At that moment I realized I was witnessing an S/M fantasy brought to life…right in the apartment across from mine. I didn't dare turn my bedroom light on for fear of being caught watching. My cock was hard as a rock between my legs as I watched the two men continue working on the bound guys nipples. I was able to see that they were heartily sucking, bighting, and kissing his nipples. The harder his cock got the worse the pain in his balls must have gotten. Then, the two guys stopped working the bound guy's nipples and again ran their hands all over his delectable chest area, slapping his pecs hard. The bound guy seemed to grunt in pain as they slapped his pecs harder and harder. My breath was coming in short gasps as the two men squatted down and reached into the metal bucket at the bound guy's feet. They each took a couple of ice cubes out of the bucket. Smiling wickedly, they rubbed the ice cubes all over the bound guy's chest, his nipples, his stomach, his arms and neck. The bound guy was shivering from the cold and when the ice cubes were small enough they pulled the bound guy's butt cheeks apart under his briefs and deposited what was left of the ice cubes into his hole. They stood there laughing mockingly as the poor stud grimaced miserably behind his blindfold. When he seemed to calm down a little they took more ice cubes out of the bucket and ran them up and down his long muscular legs, over his thighs and behind them, and over his aching balls and the sides of his hard cock. Pre cum oozed like crazy from his piss slit at that point. I didn't know which I wanted more at that moment...to be the guy who was tied up and blindfolded or to be one of the guys who were torturing him. When the ice cubes that they had been running over his legs were small and useless they once again shoved them into the bound guy's hole. Again he grimaced behind his white cloth blindfold. They took more ice cubes out of the bucket and ran them over his ass cheeks and cock at the same time. They forced a few into his mouth and made him swallow them as they shoved more and more of them into his hole. As he stood there shivering like crazy the two men took turns embracing and kissing him passionately on the lips. I could see the bound guy's tongue darting in and out of his cold mouth as he kissed the two men alternately. I wondered at that moment how long he had been standing there tied to that weight the way he was. I wondered how much he could take. The two men forced him to eat more ice cubes and by then I was wondering how badly the poor stud had to piss. To answer my question I saw one of the guys place the bucket under the bound guy's hard cock. The other guy took the bound guy's cock in his fingers and pointed it downward over the bucket. He seemed to be telling the bound guy that it was okay. Suddenly, the bound guy pissed a long and yellow stream into the bucket. I watched in awe as he seemed to piss and piss and piss...never running out of it. I guessed that if someone had shoved ice cubes up my ass and down my throat I would have to piss like crazy also. Finally, he did finish pissing and the two men again ran their hands over him, caressing him lovingly now. He seemed to be in ecstasy even though he was tied up, blindfolded, and being tortured. I watched as the two men slid to their knees in front of the bound guy and began tonguing his balls...hard. Now the bound guy was really in pain. He was arching his back and grimacing in agony at the same time. His poor balls weren't just tied and separated with a leather separator; they looked like they were filled to overflowing with jizz. The poor stud probably hadn't shot a load in more than a week. And now the two guys working him over were teasing him and making him wait. They sucked his balls into their mouths and pulled hard on them. At one point when the bound guy screamed in pain I was able to hear him even with my window closed. They ran their hands over his legs as they continued torturing his balls with their tongues. The guy bucked and arched his back in agony. When they stopped torturing his balls and stood up the guy looked like he was crying behind his blindfold. The two guys looked at each other and smiled. I could tell that they still had more torturous plans for the bound guy. One of the guys left the room and I watched as the other guy again embraced the bound and blindfolded guy. He held him close and seemed to be whispering in his ear. I would have given anything to know what he was telling him because the bound guy didn't look too thrilled at that moment. A few moments later the other guy came back into the room... carrying two round black leather paddles. He handed one to his friend and they stepped behind the bound guy. Shit, they were about to paddle that poor stud's backside. Before beginning the paddling they tore his briefs off in the back, leaving him wearing just the elastic waistband and some of what was left of the briefs he was wearing. I can't tell you just how erotic that fucker looked standing there tied the way he was wearing just the shredded remains of his briefs. One of the guys said something to the bound guy and I watched as he bent over forward as much as possible...as much as the ropes around his balls would allow actually. Now his ass was sticking out...a ready target for their paddles. The paddling began. They took turns raising their paddles and rapping his butt cheeks hard. At first the guy was just grimacing behind his blindfold but then after about twenty or so swats I could tell that he was reeling in pain. They continued paddling him...and I could tell that they were paddling him harder and harder with each blow. Sweat had started dripping off the big and muscular bound stud and he was now really in pain as they swatted his poor ass cheeks harder and harder and harder. When they finally stopped paddling him they put the paddles down squatted behind him, and ran their tongues over his balls which were pulled painfully behind him. I could see that he was not enjoying the pressure they were again applying to his very tortured balls. The way he was bent over and facing forward he would have been looking directly into my window...if he didn't have that blindfold tied over his eyes. The

two guys licked his balls like crazy, slapped his ass with the backs of
their hands, and even stuck their long fingers up in his asshole. They
squeezed his thighs and pressed their mouths against his ass cheeks.
They bit, kissed, and slurped all over his hot ass cheeks. Now he was
really fucking sweating…and not to mention it but so was I. My cock
was pounding hard but I couldn't tear myself away from watching what
they did next. One of the guys reached into the small pocket of his
leather vest and brought out what looked like a tube of Ben gay. He and
the other guy looked at each other, smiled, and they each gave the bound
guy a good hard whack on his ass. The guy holding the tube of Ben gay
opened it and smeared some of it onto his fingers. Then, the other guy
took the tube of Ben gay and did the same thing. Together, they rubbed
the Ben gay onto the bound guy's ass cheeks, up his ass, and onto his
balls. The bound guy clenched his teeth and I could see that he was in
utter agony. He was trying to stifle his screams…I guess for fear of
waking up the neighborhood. The two men each squeezed another good
dollop of the Ben gay onto their fingers and again smeared it over the
bound guy's ass cheeks, up his ass and over his by now aching balls. The
bound guy was indeed crying profusely now behind his blindfold. He
was grimacing, clenching his teeth, and I could tell that he was ready to
scream in utter agony. What he must have been feeling at that moment
God only knows. First they had rubbed ice all over him, stuck ice cubes
up his ass and down his throat and now they were heating him up,
cooking him so to speak beyond endurance. One of the guys said
something to the bound guy and he stood up straight, stopping when the
rope tugged on his aching and searing balls. The two men procceded to
rub Ben gay on his nipples, rubbing it in hard with their thumbs. As he
reeled in more pain I saw his lips move and one of the men said something
to him. He proceeded to piss again into the bucket that was still directly
under his cock. When he was done pissing the two men stopped rubbing
the Ben gay on his nipples. They stepped back to look him over and
watch as he stood there grimacing and writhing in pain. Man oh man,
the bound up muscle guy was in utter agony, totally trapped, and yet his
cock was still hard as a fucking rock. It hadn't gone down once while his
two captors were working him over. Then, one of the men said something
to him; they each kissed him on the lips, and walked out of the room,

leaving him standing there alone. I didn't move. I simply sat there looking at him as he squirmed miserably in pain. I would guess that maybe ten minutes went by and then one of the guys came back into the room. He looked the bound and blindfolded guy over, circled him a few times, and then knelt in front of him. He ran his hands over the bound guy's thighs and then slurped his cock into his mouth. The bound guy threw his head back in ecstasy as the guy sucked his cock furiously. The other guy came back a few moments later as well and knelt next to his friend. Together they took turns sucking the bound guy's cock. As they sucked him I was slowly stroking my own meat. I was in a heated frenzy. Watching all this was driving me nuts… As they went on sucking him they tugged on his aching balls and reached around him to slap his butt cheeks. The bound guy was arching his back and breathing heavily as the two men sucked him harder and harder. He was definitely as close to cumming as I was. When he shot his load one of the guys had his cock tightly in his hand as the other guy pulled on his tortured balls like crazy, squeezing them, twisting them, forcing every drop of jizz out of him. I was able to hear the bound guy's cries of passion as his sperm spewed wildly out of his cock and into the bucket at his feet. When he was done the two men let go of his cock and balls, stood up at his sides, and took turns kissing him lovingly and passionately on the lips. When I glanced down I saw that my hand was full of my cum.

The two men stopped kissing the bound guy, walked out of the room again, and came back a few seconds later this time…carrying a few lengths of rope each. What now I wondered??? The poor stud had been tortured like crazy and had shot a pretty powerful load of ball juice. What were they going to do to him now??? I watched as they wound the rope around and around his upper body, pinning his arms to his body. As they tied him even more he again threw his head back in ecstasy and his poor cock got hard again. I could only imagine the pain he must have been in as the ropes and ball separator were still around his balls. When they were done tying his upper body one of them said something to him and he leaned forward again as much as possible… exposing his bung hole for them. They pulled their big hard cocks out of their leather shorts and stepped behind him. My breath came in short gasps as they began to take turns fucking his ass. Without realizing it was jacking myself off again. The two men pounded the bound guy's ass like crazy, holding him steady by his hips as they took their turns plowing him. When they came they both shot their loads into his hole, slapping his ass cheeks as they came and came... When they were done the bound guy stood up straight and one of the men took the blindfold off him. His eyes were beautiful...brown and deep. Together, the two men untied the ropes holding the bound guy to the weight, took the ball separator off his nuts, and untied the ropes around his upper body. When he was completely untied he alternately hugged and kissed the two men who had tortured him. He kissed and kissed them both on the lips more than a few times each. Then, the two men each grabbed one of his arms and legs, hoisted him off the floor, and carried him out of the room. It appeared they were all laughing jovially. As I sat there stroking my cock and looking at the weight on the floor with the bucket of piss and cum in it in the apartment across the way the lights in that apartment went out. I guessed that one of the guys had shut the lights off after putting the stud down in the bedroom. I walked back to my bed. It was an hour and a half later. I slid back under the covers and fell back to sleep. When I woke up the next morning I quickly looked out the window and to my dismay the shade had been pulled down over the window in the apartment across the way.

On Monday morning as I was leaving for work I saw the guy who had been bound and blindfolded leaving his apartment building for work also. Like me he was dressed in a suit. As I headed for the train station he fell in next to me.

"Hi," he said to me with a grin on his exquisitely handsome face. "Did you enjoy the show?"

I looked at him in shock. That night at three AM he was again stripped naked and tied to the weight on the floor as he was that past Friday. He was blindfolded also. Everything was as it had been that Friday at three AM, except that I was now the guy about to torture him as he stood there helplessly and in pain...

A Boner Book

ANOTHER
BODY BUILDER STORY

"Ohhhhhrrrr man," I moaned, groaned and swooned as yet another fucking guy slid his tongue up into my mangy, gaping and exposed asshole. "Fucking hole munchers…"

His tongue flicked around in there like crazy, in my most private of regions I might add, driving me totally fucking batty. When he pressed his lips against the walls of my hole and began sucking it I thought that I would literally fly away… Fuck, I had lost count of how many guys had eaten, slurped, tongued, and sucked at my mangy asshole that night. I wondered how many of them had come back for second and third helpings of my very moist, very smelly, very eaten asshole. What I did know was that I was going nowhere anytime soon. I was in a slumped over position with my legs spreads wide and tied tightly to a strange sort of table. My wrists were tightly bound in front of me with mounds of rope. (Fuckers had better have tied me tightly as I'm a pro fucking bodybuilder, I fucking workout everyday of the damned week. No days off in between for yours truly here let me tell you.) My very muscular and well-toned upper body was lashed to the table. Rope had been tied over my lean iron-like thighs and each of my long and wiry thick muscled legs to hold them in place. And believe it or not rope had been tied around the sides of each of my big and round ass cheeks to hold them spread out so the men eating my hole didn't have to bother holding them open themselves. Damn, but my sexy ass cheeks sure felt numb and sore to put it bluntly. A cloth blindfold was tied over my eyes so I had no idea who the men were who were feasting repeatedly and over and over on my stink hole, and to make my situation that much worse, I had no fucking idea where I was.

"AAAARRRRHHHH Gods," I croaked as the fucking guy really went to town chowing on my damned hole. "Goddamn…"

Stinging slaps were delivered repeatedly to my spread out butt cheeks by a couple of the other men as the one eating me slurped and sucked and slurped and sucked. My big meaty and beefy cock was dangling long and semi hard between my legs, pulled through a large hole that had been cut into the table I was so thoroughly lashed to. My plum sized balls hung down along with the big guy, a rope tied just around the top of them. I have to quickly say here what a shitty thing that is to do to a poor guy, to tie up his goddamned balls, fuck!! For the moment they were leaving my cock and balls alone but earlier they too had been sucked and slurped like mad. I had been made (forced) to shoot my load numerous times and fuck, but hadn't it drove me utterly crazy when the guy had kept sucking the tip of my cock after I had shot that third creamy load of ball juice. The guy eating my hole took a few last sucks at it and then stopped. He stuck a finger deep in there and I heard the sound of men chuckling meanly. God, I imagined them all standing around the table, looking over the helpless and bound and blindfolded bodybuilder, stripped to his damned gray colored silk calf length dress socks and feasting away at his wet hole. Suddenly, I felt the awful sting of the leather paddles on my butt cheeks again.

"AWWWRRRRR no, no," I roared miserably and struggled like crazy to get untied. "Not again you bastards, don't fuckin' beat my poor cheeks again!"

They rapped my butt cheeks harder and harder with each stroke of the leather paddles, tenderizing the poor big and round globes, really putting the screws to them. This was actually the third fucking time I was being given a hard, painful, and stinging paddling. I wondered if I would cry as hard as I did with the earlier spanking I had been dealt.

"AAAYRRRRR…" I screamed, as the blows rained down on me and became harder and harder and more intense with each blow.

As my butt cheeks suffered and were being given a beating I felt the sticky and sweet honey that had been poured into my hole earlier being slopped onto my fingers with some sort of a basting brush.

"Ayyyyyrrrrrr GODS," I grunted. "What now you stinking fuckers???"

As my butt cheeks were beaten harder yet I felt my fingers suddenly being sucked like cocks, one by one. Admittedly, it felt awesome as the guy teased the tips of my honey soaked fingers with the tip of his tongue. (If you've never had someone suck at your fingers like that give it a try, you won't regret it. I only wish that you not be in the tied up predicament I was in when it was done to me.) My cock grew hard under the table and my poor balls ached from the rope tied around them. Even while being beaten my damned cock grew hard, shit! After I don't know how many harsh and stinging blows to my butt cheeks with the leather paddles, they finally stopped rapping me. Tears of anger and fear soaked my blindfold. One of the guys scurried under the table and slurped my big Spanish cock into his mouth and sucked it for all he was worth as his buddy went on sucking at my fingers. I felt a tongue slide up into my very exposed hole and I nearly spun away. Okay, one of them was sucking my fingers, one of them was sucking my cock, and one of them was again eating my hole. That made three guys, but there were more of them, somehow I could sense it. I knew there were more of them!

"Fucking guys' man," I gasped. "Why the fuck are you doing this to me???"

Fingers gripped one of my ass cheeks hard and I heard mean and fiendish chuckling. I pursed my lips as I felt myself getting close to shooting another load of creamy eggnog for them to chow down on. As I was about to cum I tried hard to think back to how the evening had begun, and how the fuck I had managed to come to be in this more than fucked up position.

It was a Friday night. The workweek was over. I had decided to have a few cold beers at a bar in my neighborhood that was called "The Local" before going to sleep that night. Also, one never knows whom one might meet at "The Local", if you catch my drift. And, being that it was the night before my birthday I felt I deserved to treat myself to a few beers. So, I shucked off my scuffed work boots, my worn jeans, my sweat soaked stinking tee shirt, and my smelly briefs and sweat socks and walked naked to the bathroom to shower before heading out to "The Local." I stunk like a football player's locker room after a big game out in the heat. My job as a construction worker helps to keep me in the finest shape possible. As the warm water cascaded over my well-built muscular body I soaped myself up, lathering up from my firm biceps and sinewy arms, running soapy fingers over my colossal chest. I gave my nipples a squeeze each and my cock jutted out in front of me, long, hard, and pulsing. My balls hung down nice and big and plump. I squeezed one of my nipples again, and with a soapy hand I grabbed my big beefy guy. Smiling, standing there under the warm water as it flowed over me, relaxing my overworked muscles, I stroked my guy slowly.

"Ohhhhhh yeah," I moaned, my deep voice echoing in the tile bathroom.

With one hand teasing one of my now very erect nipples and the other stroking my cock, I slowly led myself to orgasm. I love popping my load and I love seeing that creamy mess of ball juice erupt from my wide sexy cock slit, and at the tender age of twenty-four I have no goddamned problem getting myself off more than a few times before the day is out. Fuck, I figured that even if I did meet someone tonight at "The Local" I would still have plenty of spunk to feed the fucker after shooting my eggnog in the shower.

"Ohhhhhrrrr yeah," I grunted. "FUCKIN' A…"

I let go of my nipple, grabbed my succulent balls, and squeezed them gently as I let fly with a big load of Spanish boy spunk.

"AAAARRRHHHH yeahhhhh, yeah," I grunted wildly as I stood there with one hand stroking my big shaft and the other hand hefting my balls as I drained them.

My eyes crossed in my head and my chest jutted out real sexily as my mess splattered on the wall and dripped down into the tub…

When I was done I let the warm water massage my body a little more and then turned off the faucets. I stepped out of the shower, towel dried, and padded to the bedroom to get dressed. I pulled on a pair of fresh white briefs, gray silk calf length dress socks, a pair of charcoal colored jeans, a black tank-top, a cotton black summer jacket, and a pair of black highly shined ankle length boots. I rolled the sleeves up on my jacket in order to show off my beefy forearms, got my wallet and keys, and feeling really good and real sexy left the apartment. "The Local" is a little more than twenty blocks from my apartment, and being that it was a cool summer evening I decided to walk there, rather than take the bus. When I walked into the sleazy bar called "The Local" the place was somewhat crowded with the usual array of neighborhood guys, some guys cruising, and some who were there just for a drink before heading home after working overtime. Suits, construction workers, and everything in between came to "The Local" to kick back and relax. The smell of alcohol and cigarette smoke greeted me as I walked through the place and up to the big bar. "The Local" is a pretty big place for a neighborhood bar, dimly lit with lots of neon signs advertising different brands of beer. A pool table adorns the back end of the bar and I saw a few guys in Levis and tee shirts playing a game of pool back there. I wondered what they were playing for tonight. A quick grin passed over my face at that thought. Sometimes the guys at "The Local" played pool for money, sometimes it was for sex, other times it was drugs. Off to the side and down a short hallway was the men's room. I've had my tube steak sucked a lot in that men's room when I didn't feel like bringing the guy back to my apartment and having him spend the night with me. There's a stall in there with a big old glory hole cut into it for guys who are into that shit. One time a while back a guy sucked me for all he was worth as I stood in that stall with my pants and briefs down around my ankles and cock and balls sticking through the glory hole. Fucking guy sucked my stinking and sweaty cock and balls real fucking good let me tell you. I had come into the bar right after working all day in the grueling sun and I smelled all ripe and funky. As he sucked me the guy's hands moved over and over the exposed black dress socks I happened to be wearing that day as they climbed up out of my work boots and over my pooled down pants. In between sucking me he commented on how kinky it was that I happened to be wearing suit socks with my construction clothes. I breathlessly told him how all my sweat socks were in the laundry and that I was forced to wear the dressy socks that day. I also told him not to worry about my socks and to jus t get on with the task of sucking my cock. He happily obliged me. After the fucking guy managed to suck two hefty loads of ball juice out of me he begged me to let him have the black socks I was wearing as I stood there in front of the stall, packing my well sucked and spent cock and balls back into my jeans.

"Fuck man, you are a kinky dude," I said with a grin.

So, I leaned up against a sink, unlaced my boots, and shucked them off. The guy squatted in front of me and slid my black socks off my big feet. He stood up, sniffed the socks and then rolled them tight as I stood there bare footed. I smiled from ear to ear.

"Thanks guy," he said, patted my crotch and exited the men's room with my socks.

"Next time you should take my briefs too," I thought as I slid my now bare feet into my boots.

As I walked up to the bar I looked down the hallway at the men's room and saw a couple of guys going in there. To piss or to fool around I did not know.

"Hey Eddie," the bartender, a handsome guy named Clyde said to me as I came up to the bar. "What'll it be guy?"

"Hi Clyde," I said and shook hands with him. "Give me a twenty ounce Bud, a real cold one."

"Coming up Eddie," Clyde said and placed a can of Budweiser and a cold mug in front of me on the bar.

I handed him a ten dollar bill and he placed the change in front of me. I poured beer into the mug and took a long hearty gulp of it.

"So, how are things buddy?" Clyde asked me, his eyes looking hungrily at my chest area just visible over my tank top.

"Work is busy as usual and tomorrow I'm celebrating my twenty-sixth birthday Clyde my man," I said and held up my mug of beer.

"Hey, good for you man, happy b-day," Clyde said. "Next beer is on the house Eddie."

"Thanks Clyde," I replied with a smile and took another gulp of my beer.

I put the beer down, shucked off my jacket, and held it under my arm as I stood at the bar. I felt eyes devouring me, looking at me hungrily and lustfully. Clyde placed a tall glass of Budweiser in front of me on the bar alongside my half empty can.

"There ya go Eddie, happy b-day again man on the house," Clyde said and rushed off to serve another waiting patron.

I finished my first beer, smiled, and took a long sip of the second one. It was horribly warm and tasted like piss.

"Holy shit," I whispered and looked in Clyde's direction, wanting to ask for a better glass of beer.

He saw me looking at him and smiled over at me. I held up the glass of piss tasting beer, stupidly took another sip and grimaced. Clyde smiled at the silly look on my face. Now, as I lay tied to the table and about to shoot a fourth (fifth, sixth? I had lost count) load of eggnog for the kidnappers who had me trapped I had small flashes of memory. I placed the glass of warm piss tasting beer on the bar and my head spun. I was suddenly very dizzy and in need of a seat. I grabbed the side of the bar and I heard a voice from somewhere far away asking me if I was okay, saying that I didn't look that good at the moment. Then, fingers toying with and twisting one of my big nipples under my tank top as my vision blurred. The glass of warm piss tasting beer was held to my lips and I heard another voice telling me to drink up, that it would help me feel better in no time. I wanted to tell whoever it was that the beer was awful and that I didn't want to drink it. I was force-fed the beer and I felt a hand gripping one of my butt cheeks.

"Ohhhhhrrrrr shit," I gasped as I shot my load into the guy's mouth that was sucking me. "Fucking bastards, guys drugged me. That's how you managed to snag me."

When I was done cumming the guy at my cock slurped one of my testicles into his mouth and applied pressure to it with his tongue.

"AAAYYYRRRR!!!" I roared angrily.

The guy at my fingers had two of my digits in his mouth at the moment and the guy at my ass was slurping wildly and madly at my sopped hole.

"Fucking kidnappers, drugged my damned beer," I rasped miserably.

The guy eating my hole stopped and suddenly my butt cheeks were again being pummeled with the leather paddles.

"OOWWWWWWrrrr no, no," I yelled madly. "Not this shit again you fuckers!!"

My butt cheeks were beyond hurting at that point, they were stinging and burning with the pain. As they beat my cheeks and the guys sucked my balls and fingers my mind drifted again, back to "The Local." When the glass of awful tasting beer was empty (they had made me drink it all) I could barely stand up.

"Oh man, you're in bad shape Mister," I heard a voice say to me, again, from somewhere very far away.

My vision was totally blurred and everything looked distorted. All I saw were fuzzy images of the neon signs around the bar.

"Maybe we should get him outside so he can get some air," another far away sounding voice said.

Hands grabbed my wrists and pulled my hands off the end of the bar as I gripped it for dear life.

"N-no, I can't," I whispered and they slung my arms across their shoulders.

"Is he okay?" I heard someone ask, I think it was Clyde.

"Just had a little too much to drink," I heard someone reply. "Big guy like him you would think he could drink like a fish."

They moved me slowly across and out of the bar. The image faded again though as the fuckers really beat the tar out of my butt cheeks.

"Okay, that's enough," I heard one of the men say. "Anymore and the poor fuck will wind up bleeding all over the place."

They stopped paddling me. It was the first time I had heard any of them speak since this had all began. I was whimpering like a child and crying big tears behind my blindfold. The guy under the table now had my cock back in his mouth and was sucking it all over again. Actually, for all I knew it could have been one of the other guys down there taking a turn at my big Spanish sausage. My balls were hanging low and pulsing miserably with pain and the other guy was still sucking my damned fingers.

"Get him a drink," I heard that voice say again. "He needs to calm down."

At the sound of those words my heart leapt with terror in my big chest. Then, I felt a glass being placed to my trembling lips. I clamped my mouth shut, knowing it was the drugged beer I had been given at the bar.

"He won't drink it," I heard another voice say.

"Not a problem," the first voice said merrily. "There's another way we can make him drink it."

I felt a plastic tube being slid into my exposed asshole and then the beer was being poured through it and into my gut. Fuck, they had slid a damned household funnel into my hole.

"Oh sshiiiiittt!!!" I screeched and my head spun as it did back at the bar.

If I wasn't blindfolded I was sure my vision would have blurred as well.

My hole literally sucked up and drank the warm frothy drugged beer, as I lay there totally helpless, all of my bodybuilder strength completely useless to stop these men from using me like on suck-on toy. Unbelievably I felt myself getting ready to shoot my eggnog again. My head hit the table and more images appeared to me. Outside "The Local", I was being half walked half carried through a parking lot and over to a big van.

"Wh-whassss goin' on?" I slurred. "Wh-whaaaaa you guys thin-think you're doin'?"

I sounded totally stupid and totally drunk. Then, the back doors of the van were open and everything went black as I felt the cloth being tied over my eyes. They hoisted me into the van, keeping my hands behind me now, not wanting me to reach up and get the blindfold off. Then, my clothes being taken off me ripped off me too. They tore my tank-top off me, hands pulled my boots off my feet, and my jeans were yanked down and off me. My briefs were torn off me and I was held propped against a wall of the van as hands explored and squeezed me everywhere. My nipples were sucked and licked like crazy as was my cock and balls as I stood there wearing just my gray silk dress socks. Chills coursed through me as I was sucked on like a goddamned hard candy. I was so out of it by then that I could not speak at all though. My lips felt like they were bubbled up to twice their size. All I was able to do was stand there and be used like a sex toy. I think I shot a load for them in the van, and I think the guy sucking me swallowed it. Greedy fucks, they swallowed every shot they had sucked out of me thus far. Then, they bound me up in a hog-tied position on the floor of the van. I heard a couple of the guys get out of the van, the back doors slammed shut, and the van started moving, I guessed that the guys who had gotten out were riding up front while the others stayed in the back with me.

"Man, are you in for some real sleazy fun," I heard a voice say from inside my head and then I felt tongues licking the bottoms of my silk socked feet.

Now, the fuckers had me shooting yet another load of cream for them. As the guy sucking my cock swallowed every drop of it I moaned softly and miserably. The funnel had been taken out of my sopping wet hole and when I was done cumming the guy let my cock slip out of his mouth.

"Let's clean this hole of his before eating it again," I heard that echoed voice say. "We don't want to accidentally drink any of the beer we gave him."

I heard chuckling and then an ice cube was pressed against my hole.

"Ohhhhh no, no, not this again," I rasped more to myself than out loud.

They slid the ice cube all over my hole, their fingers prodding it in between the cleaning it was getting. I shivered from the cold and their touch under the tight and binding ropes as the ice cube was run over my very exposed and very eaten up hole. The guy had stopped sucking my fingers, as there was no more honey on them for him to suck off. But then, when my hole was spic and span clean I felt the sticky honey being slopped in there and again my hole was being feasted upon like it was the main course at a buffet.

"Fuck," I whispered. "Honeyed up my hole again eh? Bet it tastes real fucking good back there…"

As the guy slurped and sucked my hole again my mind once more drifted to how all this had begun. I suddenly recalled the van I was hog-tied in coming to a stop. The back doors opened and I heard men chuckling mockingly.

"Shit, look at you guys, licking his damned feet," one of the guys who had been up front said laughingly. "How do those socks of his taste huh?"

"Can't fucking leave him alone man," one of the men sucking my socked toes said and snapped the elastic in one of my socks against my calf.

"Well come on, let's get him inside," I heard the first voice say.

Then, I was being lifted and carried out of the van. I guessed that we were in a garage that was connected to a house. That was the only way they could get me from the van to the house totally unseen. I mean most people who happened to see a bound, blindfolded guy wearing just his socks being carted into a house by a group of kidnappers would most surely call the police. And to carry a bodybuilder like me there had to be more than three or four of the men. Once in the house they undid the hog-tie I was in but left me blindfolded as they proceeded to rope me to the table I was now on. I was still pretty woozy from the drugged beer I had drunk so I was not able to stop them from tying me securely to the table and spreading my legs wide. Before they started eating and slurping at my damned hole they each ran an ice cube against it, driving me crazy with the cold, cleaning me out back there with the cubes and what felt like paper towels. The way my cock and balls were hanging freely down under the table I knew that there had to be a large hole carved into it, just for that sleazy purpose.

"Wha-wah you guys want?" I asked in a drunken slur as they continued pressing ice cubes against my hole and delivering open handed slaps to my big round ass cheeks.

I received no reply however, except more hard open handed slaps on my butt cheeks. The sounds of the slaps I was receiving resounded through the room they had me in.

"Fuckers, kidnapped me…" I whispered miserably.

When my hole was cleaned to their satisfaction I felt the first helping of the sticky and sweet honey being smeared in there with various fingers. They stuck their fingers into my hole as they slopped the honey in and out of it, preparing a treat for them. I then felt the first tongue lapping hungrily and maddeningly at my hole and I nearly jumped out of my skin. I yelped and goose bumps broke out all over me. Other tongues were licking and kissing my tied spread out ass cheeks and one of the guys went under the table to gobble my big sausage sized cock into his mouth. As I was sucked and licked I realized that they were treating me like a damned buffet. When all the honey had been licked out of my hole they smeared another good helping into it and took turns licking and sucking it out. The guy under the table went on sucking me until I shot a good hefty sized load of eggnog for him to swallow. He gulped down my juices, sucking at the tip of my cock only now, really making my head spin. When the second helping of honey was all eaten out of my hole I was given the first of various hard and painful stinging spankings with what I surmised to be their leather paddles. Believe me; nothing stings the ass like a leather paddle when one is being spanked with it. As I was spanked good and fucking hard and screaming in pain another guy found his way under the table, tugged my balls down low, tied a rope around the top of them, and slurped my semi hard organ into his eager cock sucking mouth.

"OHHHHRRRRR shit, don't fuckin' suck me off again so soon you fuckers," I grunted as chills and pain coursed through me.

So there I was, a fucking muscle bound super-strong dude, totally helpless, tied down, blindfolded, stripped to my goddamned socks, and having my asshole and cock repeatedly sucked. As I said earlier, I had no fucking idea where I was or who the men were that had me trapped in such a mortifying and horrifying way. They were again taking turns licking and slurping at my hole and my head spun from the warm drugged beer that they had funneled in there.

"OHHHHRRRRR GODS," I moaned throatily as I felt one of them under the table licking at the very tip of my cock.

"Okay guys, lets get this muscle boy off one more time and then we'll give him what he really needs," I heard the guy under the table say and then he slurped me meanly into his mouth.

"OOOOOOOOOO!!!!" I swooned.

He sucked me up to a new hard-on as the other guys kept taking turns eating, licking, and slurping at my hole. My cock was feeling sore and numb at that point and it took quite a while before I shot a small spurt of eggnog for the cock sucker under the table to feast on, his tongue teasing my cock slit even after I had come.

"AAAYYYRRRRRR..." I grunted wildly as they drove me practically insane.

When I was done shooting my load for what felt like the umpteenth time the guy let my cock slip out of his mouth. I lay there huffing, heaving, and gasping for breath as they stopped eating my hole. I was a sweaty and stinking mess and feeling totally woozy and used up.

"Feelin' good?" one of the men asked me and gave each of my ass cheeks a squeeze each.

"Y-yeah, just great," I whimpered and managed to lift my head up off the table. "Just what I've always dreamed of, bein' kidnapped and treated like a buffet table at an all night sex party…"

Suddenly, the blindfold was whisked off me and as my eyes adjusted to the light I looked up at my captors.

"Ho-holy shit!! Holy fucking shit!!" I said loudly and a wicked smile came across my lips as relief filled me. "Oh holy fuck, you fucking guys!!"

Looking up, I saw six of my work buddies from the job. Ron, Steve, Lenny, Kevin, Danny, and Angel were all standing around the table with their big cocks sticking out of their jeans.

"Happy Birthday Eddie!!" they said loudly in unison.

I laughed along with them, loving the birthday joke they had managed to play on me. They gave my ass a few hard slaps each and prodded my wet hole with their fingers. "Fucking guys, best buddies a guy could ever have," I said with a grin on my face. "But was it really necessary to paddle the fuck out of my poor cheeks?"

"Just think of them as birthday paddles," Ron, the ringleader as always said and ruffled my dark hair.

Lenny tied the blindfold back over my eyes and for the remainder of the party I had to guess which of them was fucking my very lubricated hole. For each wrong guess I was paddled again… Overall, it was actually the best fucking birthday party I ever had, a party that went on all fucking night as my buddies fucked the tar out of me, ate my hole again and again, and forced me to shoot still more gobs of Spanish eggnog for them. Thanks guys…

ABOUT THE AUTHOR

Christopher Trevor was born in July 1963 and grew up in New York City. As soon as he was old enough to know how he began writing fiction and has been writing gay erotic/fetish stories for the past ten to twelve years at this point. He became an avid reader as well from the time he knew how and reads everything from fiction, to non-fiction to biographies of interesting and unusual people, people who have made a difference or who have paved the way for others. Christopher attributes his writing artistic inspiration to artists such as Etienne, Tom of Finland, Tagame, The Hun, and most notably Joe T, who Christopher has had the pleasure of speaking with and even meeting over the last few years. Christopher states, "Joe T encouraged me to write about my fetish because I was embarrassed about it at the time. Joe T said that when we are embarrassed about something that makes it even more enticing somehow." Christopher totally agreed and never stopped writing in this genre. Erotic writers who inspired Christopher Trevor were: Tom Shaw (author of "That Day at the Quarry), C.S. White (author of Big Sur), Larry Townsend (author of countless erotic novels), and Mason Powell (author of the classic story "The Brig.")

Christopher discovered that not only did he enjoy writing erotic tales but that after his first bondage experience he had a genuine flair for it. Writing to erotic oriented magazines about his first bondage experience truly opened the floodgates for Christopher where this style of writing is concerned. Christopher thanks the handsome and muscular "Greg" for that experience way back in time. Christopher took "Creative Writing" courses every semester during his high school years and while other friends of his stopped writing what they loved to write about as time went on Christopher never let a day go by when he didn't write something... "I feel that if I don't write every day I will die," Christopher has said many times over.

Foot fetish stories and all things related; spanking fetish, erotic shaving, muscle bondage, tickle torture, and hardcore stories are just a few of the areas of gay eroticism that Christopher enjoys writing about and inspiring in others as well. As one internet buddy said to Christopher where the black socks fetish is concerned, "Until I started talking with you I never gave a thought to my socks when I got dressed for work in the morning. Now when I pull my dress socks on every morning I get a chill up my spine."

Christopher is proud of the erotic effect he has on people...

Christopher Trevor is also the author of:

The Executive Guide to Foot Fetishism and Office Discipline
    1-887895-36-1

Executive Ties That Bind
    1-887895-37-X

Don't!! Stop!! That Tickles!!
    1-887895-31-0

The Taming of Dominick
    1-887895-45-0

Timmy and The Hong Kong Tailor
1-887895-30-2

Love, Torture and Redemption
1-887895-32-9

Timmys Ticklish Trials
978-1-887895-74-3

The Gym Instructor
978-1-887895-44-6

Milked
978-1-887895-66-8

Erotic Street Blues
978-1-887895-97-2

The Abusive Wager
978-1-887895-04-0

Terry's Appointment and Other Tickling Stories
978-1-934625-08-8

Look for them where you bought this book or Goodboner.com.

Made in the USA
Lexington, KY
16 October 2011